SOLYRIAN CONSPIRACY

SOLYRIAN CONSPIRACY

THE RISE OF MAGIC™ BOOK NINE

CM RAYMOND   LE BARBANT   MICHAEL ANDERLE

LMBPN

DISRUPTIVE IMAGINATION®

This book is a work of fiction. All of the characters, organizations, and events portrayed in this novel are either products of the author's imagination or are used fictitiously. Sometimes both.

Copyright © 2019 C.M. Raymond, LE Barbant & Michael Anderle
Cover by Mihaela Voicu http://www.mihaelavoicu.com/
Cover copyright © LMBPN Publishing
A Michael Anderle Production

LMBPN Publishing supports the right to free expression and the value of copyright. The purpose of copyright is to encourage writers and artists to produce the creative works that enrich our culture.

The distribution of this book without permission is a theft of the author's intellectual property. If you would like permission to use material from the book (other than for review purposes), please contact support@lmbpn.com. Thank you for your support of the author's rights.

LMBPN Publishing
PMB 196, 2540 South Maryland Pkwy
Las Vegas, NV 89109

First US edition, December, 2019
Version 1.02, December 2019
ebook ISBN: 978-1-64202-661-0
Print ISBN: 978-1-64202-662-7

The Kurtherian Gambit (and what happens within / characters / situations / worlds) are copyright © 2015-2020 by Michael T. Anderle and LMBPN Publishing.

THE SOLYRIAN CONSPIRACY TEAM

Thanks to our JIT Readers

Micky Cocker
Diane L. Smith
Jackey Hankard-Brodie
Dorothy Lloyd
Peter Manis
Nicole Emens
Paul Westman
Shari Regan
Dave Hicks
James Caplan
Lori Hendricks

Editor

SkyHunter Editing Team

"It's beautiful. Freaking beautiful," Hannah said, looking out over the bow of the *Unlawful* at the sun setting as they sailed over unknown lands. As each day passed, the girl from the Boulevard saw the breadth of diverse places the world had to offer.

"Aye, 'tis." Karl sighed as his eyes traced the pinks and purple exploding across the horizon, painting the rolling hills like a tapestry. "It makes me want ta—"

The ship lurched to starboard, and Karl instantly turned green. Lunging, he shoved his head across the rail and expelled his dinner, ale and all, directly overboard. Standing again, he leaned against the wood and wiped his mouth with the back of his hand.

Hannah tried to stop laughing, but the look on the rearick's face made it impossible. "You're really touched by this sunset."

"*Scheisse!* Lass, I'll be good and damned if that kid doesn't learn ta drive the bloody boat. I'd give a nut to get

Gregory back behind them controls, even for just a day. Maybe both of them nuts of mine."

"Not much of a sacrifice." Hannah grinned. "It's not like you use them all that often."

Karl's face turned from green to red.

"I'm just kidding," she said, still grinning like a rabid remnant. "Aysa is doing just fine, Karl."

"Aye. In fact, I'm pretty sure the little freak is just screwin' with me. Ye know she gets off on that. She's had it out fer me since the day we met."

Hannah turned and looked back over the landscape. "And Gregory... We all wish he was here. Him *and* the others."

Karl grimaced as he kept his eyes on the fixed land below. "Well, Hannah, I do always forget yer still a little green in the ways of war."

"Funny, *you* calling *me* green, Sir Pukes-A-Lot."

He waved her off and continued, "The members of a company come and go as needed. It's the way it is in the life we've chosen."

"Or that's chosen us."

"Aye. We should be nothin' but glad fer Laurel and Gregory. They can raise that little bundle of joy they borned like he ought to be brought up. Not out here in gods know where. Their baby Zeke has a chance at somethin' like a normal childhood in New Romanov. Anyway, with Lilith gallivantin' the universe with ol' Gray Beard, we need Gregory back there to keep an eye on that nasty old rift. Block them red-faced creeps out of our world once and fer all."

"Again, who are you calling red-faced?" Hannah

grabbed Karl's shoulder for a squeeze. Nobody could handle deprecation better than the rearick, but still, it was important to her that Karl know she had nothing but love for him. "I know who you really miss."

A grin spread on Karl's face. Ever since the Bitch and Bastard Brigade had formed, he had been the veteran of the crew. There was only one other who had nearly as much experience in life and war. "Nah. The only thing a mystic is good fer is parlor tricks. But sure, I miss Hadley as much as ye do, I reckon. But 'tis good he headed back to the Heights. That sonofabitch needs ta get his head straight, after all."

Hannah nodded. Hadley was the closest thing to a brother she'd had since William was killed in the Boulevard. Hadley had trained her and walked her through the growing pains of developing all aspects of her magic, especially mental magic. But ever since he had melded minds with Laughter, the residue of her residence in his brain had never quite been wiped clean. Fever dreams had littered his sleep, and shadows marked his waking life. It had taken some goading, but finally Hannah had convinced him it was time to return home, to the mystics' compound in the Heights, where powerful teams of magicians might be able to fix the deep cracks in his mind.

"Had will be fine, and we're going to be just fine without him. I mean, at least we've got this guy with us." She nodded toward the stern where two figures engaged in combat were silhouetted in the evening sky. One man advanced toward the other, who held a spear with a glowing blue tip.

"Ye mean yer little love bug or Cat Scratch Fever?"

Hannah laughed. "Well, I meant Vitali. But I hope they both make it through the journey. The way the two of them are sparring daily, I'm shocked neither have been cast overboard yet. But they're getting tougher every bloody day."

Just as she finished, Parker jumped back onto the cabin roof. With the ease of a gymnast, he leapt over the Lynqi's head. Landing, he swept out his partner's legs with a graceful spin. The furred fighter was back on his feet before Parker could advance for a finishing move.

"Aye, only difference between Vitali and a cat is that he's got nine hundred lives."

The edges of Hannah's mouth turned up in a proud grin. "They're getting good."

"Aye. Real damned good."

"Want to show them how to really fight?"

Karl rolled his neck. "Never thought ye'd ask. Let's show them what—" Before Karl could finish, a crash resounded from below deck, and the massive ship creaked and tremored. "The hell was that?"

"Let's go." Hannah took off for the hatch, and Karl churned his short legs as fast as he could to keep pace all the way to the cockpit. Aysa looked up as the door slammed open.

"Everything's all right up here?" Hannah asked.

"Fine as far as I know." Aysa looked at Karl. "But you might want to keep an eye on your friend here. The rearick looks a little peaked."

"Screw ye, Long Arms. I know what yer up ta. And when we land this thing, I'm gonna take that impish little smile off yer face and—"

"Down, boy," Hannah said. She looked at Aysa. "What the hell was that crash?"

Aysa shrugged and pointed toward the back of the ship. "Came from back there."

A knowing look crossed Hannah's face, and she and Karl said in unison, "Sal!"

Taking their time, they walked toward the mess. Karl braced himself, a hand on either wall of the passage as the ship lurched. "She's doing it again."

Hannah ignored him and crossed the threshold into the mess. Everything was as it ought to be. The table that extended down one end of the hall. The dark kitchen off the back. The curtains were drawn over the windows, just as they had been last time she was there. Everything was as it ought to be. Everything except for the giant dragon in the middle of the room, lying on his back with his legs extended like stiff poles up toward the ceiling.

Hannah rounded Sal's scaled body and made her way toward his head, which slumped to the side. The dragon's eyes were closed, and his mouth gaped open, his long lizard tongue hanging from between his razor-sharp teeth.

"Looks like Sal's dead," Karl said. "*Again.*"

Hannah crouched by her dragon and ran a nail along his neck and up under his chin. She could feel his body quiver under her touch. Playing dead was a trick Sal had learned from a particularly large dog several hundred miles north of their present course in a small town they had stopped at for a few days. He now used it almost every day to get what he wanted.

She shook her head. "You think we should just toss him overboard?"

"*Scheisse*, lass. That would be a waste of a lot of good meat if ye ask me. He couldn't have been down fer long. Imma guess the flesh ain't gone sour yet. If I sharpen me axe, I could carve the old lizard into steaks before ye could say 'the Matriarch.'" He paused, looking down on the beast. "How do ye like yer reptile? Medium rare? If ye roll him, I could get a mighty juicy tenderloin, I expect."

"Hmmm." Hannah narrowed her eyes. "I hear dragon is as tough as remnant meat and tastes even worse. Maybe we can revive the bag of bones."

"Ye mean, magic?" Karl asked her with a wink.

"I mean the magic of the Dark Forest." Hannah turned to the pantry and pulled out a pot holding the remainder of the kaffe they had brewed after dinner. Sal opened one eye and locked it on his master. The rest of him lay perfectly still. Hannah glanced at Karl and back at Sal. "I think it might just work."

The mighty beast snapped both eyes open and rolled onto his haunches, his entire body trembling in anticipation.

"Chill the hell out, Sal," Hannah told him. "First, a reminder of the rules."

The dragon nodded, his tail wagging across the dusty floor.

"Ye must stay off the damned boat." Karl grunted, and Sal nodded again in response. "Or no more kaffe fer ye. And I mean, *ever*."

Hannah fought off her smile, feigning severity with her dragon. "No coming back onto the ship until you are *sure* the kaffe is out of your system. We don't want a repeat of the last time. Gregory isn't here to fix your destruction, and I bet he is still whining to Laurel about the hole you put in the stern."

Sal wagged his tail more rapidly, his eyes darting between Hannah and Karl, pleading for the sweet, sweet nectar his blood craved. Hannah wished she could have made a creature without such an addiction to the druid's brew.

"And if ye mess up this time, no more of the devil elixir fer a month or two. Got it?"

Sal's head sprang up and down like bobber on a lake. Hannah tried not to laugh as she held out the pot. Her dragon's chin tilted back, mouth open, as he waited for his fix. Pouring a little less than a pint in, she shot back toward a wall with Karl on her heels. In the middle of the room, Sal stood statue-still for a beat while the kaffe worked its way from his stomach into his bloodstream.

Karl took his last chance for an admonition. "Rules, dragon!"

Sal's head tilted toward the deck before shooting up again. He began to spin like a dog chasing its tail.

"*Scheisse*, lass. Ye gave him a bit much."

Hannah pointed at the door. "Out!" she screamed. The dragon shot for the door. Floorboards creaked as he chugged down the hall, up the stairs, and out into the evening sky.

Karl shook his head. "By me hammer, I've no idea why ye want ta give that overgrown lizard kaffe."

Hannah shrugged. "A little jitter juice never harmed a thing."

"Except the *Unlawful's* hull, a grain elevator in Kaskara, a pauper's oxcart on the road to Masteran, and poor old

Ms. Sofya's ninetieth birthday cake at what was probably her last party. So, sure, lass, I guess yer little pet never bothered a thing."

"Karl, for a rearick who likes to drink himself under the table, you can be a real buzz kill, you know that?"

"Aye, well, ye never know what could happen to yer unnatural creation. There's nothin' more predictable than a piss-drunk rearick under the table, but a dragon? Well, ye sure as hell don't know what—" A crash down the hall interrupted Karl's rant.

"Sal!" he and Hannah shouted as they sprinted out of the room.

In the hall, there was no sign of the dragon. There was nothing but a booted leg lying across the threshold of the pilot's cockpit.

"The bloody hell is that?" Karl asked as he trudged down toward the mystery appendage. "I know the freak from Baseek is huge, but that thar foot is monstrous."

"Where I'm from, my feet are dainty," Aysa said, stepping over the boot. "Nothing like that brute."

"Aysa, who is that?" Hannah asked.

The girl shrugged. "No clue, but I think I surprised him. Oh, and I think we're being boarded."

CHAPTER TWO

Vitali leaned back, watching as Parker's spear passed mere inches from his face. There were risks involved in training with real weapons, but Karl always said spending too much time practicing with dull blades made dull fighters.

And Vitali needed to be the sharpest fighter possible.

He ducked and moved forward. Parker had the advantage of reach, but that advantage disappeared if Vitali could get inside the arc of the Arcadian's spear. Then Vitali's knives would prove to be the superior weapons.

It wasn't as if Team BBB needed another fighter. Everyone on board could hold their own, and then some. Plus, their captain just might be the most powerful being on the planet. But Vitali hated being the weak link, and other than his claws, he had little to offer.

Aysa could pilot and maintain the ship. Parker was a tactical genius. Karl's commands were as powerful as his hammer. And Hannah…

Well, Hannah could move mountains.

But Vitali, what did he have to offer? Back in Kaskara, Vitali was a person of significance. The son of the village *glavne*, an influential warrior. But his village was small compared to the vastness of Irth. Out here, he was one blade among many, albeit, a much furrier one.

Parker saw the attack coming. He spun aside and swept outward with the butt of his spear, keeping his distance from the cat.

"Can't catch me that easily."

"Dance all you want, Arcadian," Vitali purred. "I've got the patience of a river. A river who is about to sweep right over your ass."

Parker smiled, holding his spear at the ready. "Then prove it, furball."

Vitali knew Parker was goading him. Vitali's usual style was to stay on the defensive and wait for his opponent to make a mistake, then slip in for the kill. Parker's taunts never cracked the Lynqi's thick skin. But today, Vitali decided to change things up.

With a snarl, he leapt forward, his powerful legs launching him like coiled springs. Parker, as Vitali had hoped, was taken off-guard by the ferocity of the sudden attack. He held his spear parallel as a shield, a move Vitali expected. He dropped his knives and grabbed Parker's spear.

But Parker had plans of his own.

He fell backward and dropped the spear, letting Vitali's momentum carry him overhead. The catman landed hard on the deck. He tried to roll to his feet, but the *Unlawful* pitched severely, and he couldn't stop himself from slamming into one of the ship's outer walls.

Vitali caught his breath. He looked out over the vast valley forest below them and saw something that made even less sense to his mind than the flying ship.

A small army of people clinging to the sides of that ship. And climbing.

He heard a gentle thud as first one arrow, then another and another embedded themselves in the *Unlawful's* hull. Thick ropes hung from the arrows, and Vitali's keen eyes could make out small figures quickly ascending.

He turned around to find a smiling Parker, who was currently spinning Vitali's knives.

"Wanna trade?" Vitali asked.

"Why," Parker said. "Don't you think you're as good with a spear as I am with these knives?"

"No, because I don't know how to shoot the damn thing, and we're going to need it. We're under attack."

CHAPTER THREE

Karl burst onto the deck, hammer in hand and quickly assessed the situation. Parker and Vitali were back to back, currently holding their own against a half-dozen fighters in long, dark clothing. They wielded short spears and small shields like Aysa's, and they knew how to use them. But despite the coordinated effort of the attack, they seemed to fight as individuals rather than as a unit.

Which meant they'd be no match for Team BBB.

Karl quickly floored a man running toward him, then spun to take down another. As he did, a shadow passed overhead. He looked up to see a woman with wings soar above him.

"Bloody hell."

A second later, the woman and her wings had burst into flames. She screamed as she sailed over the edge of the ship.

He turned to see Hannah emerge, red eyes glowing in the night.

"It looks like we're having a party, and I wasn't invited."

"Yeah, well, ye always ruin the fun."

Hannah smiled and hurled a spear of ice into a man climbing over the rail of the ship. "People like my party tricks."

"I assure ye that guy did NOT like yer tricks."

Several more shadows passed overhead, but as Hannah's fireballs torched the large wings, something strange happened. The people attached to those wings let go and landed on the deck, spears at the ready.

"They're using some sort of damn kites."

"Manmade wings...brilliant," Hannah said, her silver knife zipping around her like it had a mind of its own.

"Attacking this ship? Not so much. Where the bloody hell are they comin' from?"

Hannah looked toward the mountains. "One way to find out. You good up here?"

"Aye," Karl said. "The boys and I will be fine. We'll hold the deck and keep 'em from gettin' inside. What are ye gonna do?"

Hannah smiled. "I'm going to go crash a party." A flash of light lit the deck, and then she was gone.

The spear-wielding pirates stood back in awe, but the confusion didn't last. They saw that the only thing standing between them and the door that led into the *Unlawful* was one tiny man...and they were clearly unaware of the existence of rearick.

Karl tightened his grip on his hammer. It felt good to stretch his arms.

The pirates fell before him. Their outfits and weapons

were good for boarding a flying ship at night but bad for taking down a battle-hardened mountain-dweller bearing a hammer. He could see Vitali and Parker still working as a team as they slashed and stabbed the would-be thieves. Those two young men could tangle with the best of them, and Karl was beginning to think this night would be over quickly.

Until a mountain of a man landed on the deck.

Most of the pirates were short and lean, and this man easily stood taller than the rest. He nearly rivaled Aysa for height, and his arms bulged under the dark fabric.

Karl didn't see the kite that had carried him, but it must have been huge.

The trespasser didn't hesitate. He hurled his spear like a missile. Karl barely got his hammer up in time to block it. The pirate smiled a broad toothless grin as he pulled two axes from his belt. "You show some spirit, little man. I will show you the kindness of killing you before I throw you from this ship."

"Aye, and I'll show ye the kindness of cleaning me hammer before I ram it down yer throat."

The pirate charged, moving strangely fast for his size. Usually, a hammer like Karl's was made for breaking shields and caving in breastplates, not parrying a two-handed attack, and the pirate whirled and hacked with his hatchets like he had used them to cut down hundreds of men.

But hundreds of men didn't hold a candle to Karl.

Using his short stature to his advantage, he aimed his hammer low. The pirate was quick on his feet, but all it took was one unexpected lurch of the ship for Karl to sweep those quick feet with his hammer. The large man shook the deck as he fell.

Before Karl could move in to finish the kill, a half-dozen fighters with spears descended upon him, pushing to get through the door. As he fought back against the fray, Karl caught a last glimpse of the huge man as he limped toward the edge of the ship and pulled himself overboard.

"Next time, ye oversized pirate dipshite."

CHAPTER FOUR

Hannah landed in the middle of an old pine forest. There were men and women running in every direction, working on loading giant ballistae. The large mounted crossbows lined the valley floor, firing bolt after bolt toward the *Unlawful*. Thick cords traveled behind, giving the fighters a line to climb.

She couldn't help but smile. It was the exact plan her team of resistance fighters had once used to steal the ship from Adrien, but these poor souls wouldn't be nearly as lucky as they had been. No one seemed to notice Hannah, so she decided to change that. She knelt and drove her fingers into the soil, and within seconds, trees around her were exploding, raining shards of bark, limbs, and needles like shrapnel down on the army.

That caught their attention.

"I'm going to give you one chance to pack up and get the hell away from my ship," she shouted.

Two men with bright yellow sashes across their chests, obviously commanders of some kind, stared at her, then at each other, and finally at their men. They barked an order, and two dozen fighters ran toward her.

"Have it your way." She shrugged.

These people obviously knew how to fight, but they were in no way prepared for Hannah's blend of magic and martial ferocity. She moved through the attacking force like she was cutting grass. Within minutes, twenty people lay dead or dying at her feet. The lucky ones were cut down by her knife or impaled by melting spears of ice. The unlucky ones were broken by her bare hands.

There were some advantages to having the blood of a goddess running through your veins.

The two yellow-sashed commanders stood back in fear as Hannah took a menacing step toward them, but to their credit, they didn't flee. Instead, they readjusted their attack. Two ballistae swung in her direction.

"Fire!" they shouted in unison, launching missiles thick enough to level a castle wall.

Hannah caught the bolts, one in each hand. She closed her eyes and forced her magic into them, using her physical alchemy to change their makeup, along with the physical structure of the ropes running from them back toward the commanders.

Hannah opened her eyes and smiled.

"You wanted fire? You got it."

Flames burst from her hands and raced along the magically altered ropes. The two men had just long enough to imagine their fate before the flames reached the ballistae. An explosion ripped through the side of the mountain, sending men screaming, with flames licking around their bodies. The whole army turned to stare at Hannah and the damage she had wrought.

A hundred spears pointed toward her. She merely drew her knife and smiled.

The blood of the Matriarch came with many, many bonuses.

CHAPTER FIVE

"This is almost too easy," Parker shouted as he used his magitech spear to shoot down another hang-glider. "It's like hunting pigeons."

"My people use nets for hunting birds," Vitali said as he ended a man with a fluid motion of his knives. "Not that strange machine you call a spear. And besides, there isn't much honor in shooting down pigeons."

Parker laughed. "A bad metaphor, then, because these pigeons have spears of their own, and they're trying to kill us. Luckily, my spear is *way* better than their impotent sticks."

As Parker laughed his way through the melee, a woman on a hang-glider dove toward him. Most of the fighters dropped from their kites and fell on them, but this one was smarter. She angled her kite low and directly toward him. He turned his spear toward her, but at the last minute, the *Unlawful* lurched, a shift that didn't affect the air-born attacker. Parker stumbled and the woman slammed into his shoulder, sending him reeling.

The next thing he knew, he was over the edge.

Parker screamed as the side of the *Unlawful* raced past him. He reached out to grab one of the ropes hanging from the ship, but his hand missed by inches.

This is it, he thought. *I'm finished.*

He closed his eyes and waited for the ground, but it never came. Instead, a sharp pain cut through his shoulders, halting his fall.

He turned to see a furry hand with sharp claws sinking into his arm.

"Why is it that I'm always saving you from falling to your death?" Vitali asked as he hung from the rope. "Do Arcadians not know how to hold on?"

Parker laughed, mostly out of relief. "It's definitely an oversight in our education. Good thing we have a Lynqi on board."

Parker slung his spear onto his back, and with Vitali's help, he was able to swing over to the rope. Then the two started the long climb back onto the ship.

"We had better hurry," Vitali said. "Karl is on deck all by himself, and it doesn't look like this attack is slowing down."

Parker followed Vitali's eyes downward toward the valley. He could see black-cloaked figures climbing the rope behind him.

"Maybe I can do something about that," Parker said. He pulled his spear back out and held it against the rope. "See you later."

With his spear as a crossbar, Parker slid down the rope, using it as a zipline. The face of the first fighter he met was priceless as his boots slammed into it.

CHAPTER SIX

Vitali stared in awe as Parker barreled through a line of climbing invaders. Everywhere they went, strangers assumed Vitali was an animal, but every human he traveled with was ten times as wild as he had ever been.

Continuing his climb, he soon reached the hull of the *Unlawful*. Vitali wondered how the pirates continued their ascent after reaching the end of the rope, so he watched as an attacker on a line a dozen feet from him pulled two small knives from his belt and used them to climb with.

Vitali smiled as he bared his claws. Nature had given him a better way.

His plan was to reach the deck and help Karl any way he could, but that plan fell to pieces as he saw the invaders attempting a new plan. They were cutting a hole directly into the side of the ship. Vitali made a beeline for that spot, clinging tightly to the hardened wood with his claws. Another large dip by the *Unlawful* nearly threw him, but he redoubled his efforts when he realized what the ship's erratic movements meant.

The pirates had reached Aysa.

He had to move fast.

Vitali judged the distance, then leapt toward the nearest rope. With one hand he grabbed tightly, and with the other, he used his knife to hack at the cord beneath his grip. The ten men or so climbing beneath him plummeted to the ground, but Vitali had no time to worry about them. Cut loose from its anchor, the rope he held swung wildly in the wind. Vitali kicked his legs out, using his momentum to angle him toward the open hole in the hull. He came in fast and a little low but managed to clear the distance with one last leap. His claws grabbed the edge of the ship, and he pulled himself inside.

The hallway before him was dark, but with his cat-like eyes, he could see it was empty. He ran, forsaking his normal caution when he heard the sounds of a fight below deck. Two turns and he was inside the cockpit, watching as the one-armed Baseeki tried to fight off three invaders while simultaneously piloting the airship. Her whirling bolas kept the men at bay.

"The first one who tries for these controls gets their jaw smashed to bits!"

From the look on Aysa's face, it was clear she meant it.

Vitali decided not to waste the distraction Aysa offered. He dropped one man before he was even aware of the Lynqi's presence, but the man's death rattle gave away the game.

A woman with shoulders broader than Karl's turned toward him with her shield up and her spear pointed out, a smart defensive position that made sense in the tight confines of the ship's cockpit. Vitali preferred fighting outdoors, where ample space gave him room to work his speed and agility to his advantage, but he could kill inside easy enough.

The woman stabbed at him, hoping his unarmed body would fall to her spear, but Vitali was ready. He dodged, then pounced, using the exact move he had tried on Parker just minutes earlier. But this woman was no Parker, and Vitali's knives found their home.

Practice makes perfect, he thought.

As she fell to the deck, Aysa used her bolas to disarm her attacker before smashing the hard metal balls into the man's face.

"Nice move," Vitali said.

Aysa nodded, grinning. "Thanks for the assist. Any more of them out there?"

Vitali checked the hall, then shook his head. "Looks like they're giving up."

Aysa laughed. "That tends to happen when people run headfirst into the living, breathing hellfire of a broad that is our boss."

CHAPTER SEVEN

Hannah walked around the forest, making sure the attacking army was neutralized. If there were any threats left, they weren't showing their heads.

Her fireballs tended to have that effect on people.

As she stepped around the shattered remains of a ballista, a man's body slammed to the ground in front of her with a thud, his body denting it. She wondered idly if she had thrown someone into the air, but then she looked up and saw Parker falling right behind him.

Hannah reached out, willing her magic to slow his fall. It worked just enough so that she could catch him before he hit.

He stared at her in shock before looking down at the way she cradled him in her arms like a newborn.

"Not my most manly moment."

"I'd have to agree with you there," she said, setting him on his feet. "Why were you falling out of the sky, anyway?"

"I, uh…" Parker looked at the dead bodies surrounding her. "I came to rescue you."

Hannah leaned in and kissed him. "My hero."

Sal thumped to the ground a second later, nearly taking them out as he landed.

"And where the hell were you?" she said. "There were killers on kites. We could have used a flying dragon of our own."

Sal bowed his head in mock apology, but Hannah could tell by the way his tail wagged anxiously that he was still enjoying his kaffe high. She laughed as she scratched behind his ears. "Your addiction is getting in the way of your duties, big guy."

"I don't know." Parker smirked. "I think I see pirate-flesh in his teeth. All hopped up on kaffe? My guess is he did more damage than you."

"Is that right?" Hannah asked, scratching harder. "Man's best friend, right here."

While she tended to her dragon, Parker poked one of the dead bodies. "Who the hell are these guys, anyway? Is there someone with a grudge against us in these parts?"

Hannah thought for a second, then shook her head. "There is now, but they'd have to be pretty freaking stupid to try anything else against us. My guess is they had scouts who marked our airship from a distance, then simply waited for us to arrive. This valley is the perfect ambush spot."

Parker nodded. None of this was too shocking. A vessel like the *Unlawful* was something of a rarity in Irth, and everywhere Team BBB went, people either fled in terror from it or tried to take it from them. Hannah simply chalked it up to the risks associated with air travel.

Parker picked up one of their spears and tested th

balance for a second before dropping it to the ground. "You want to investigate further? They probably have some sort of village or base nearby."

Hannah considered it for a moment before shaking her head. "Does it make me a bad hero of Irth if I say no? I'd say we taught them a mighty powerful lesson today, one they're not likely to forget anytime soon. Let's just get back to the ship."

Parker smiled. "I can't speak to your 'hero of Irth status,' but I think it makes you human—regardless of the Queen Bitch's blood in your veins."

Hannah smiled, then gave Parker another kiss. "Sweet talk like that is all I need from a man."

They climbed onto Sal's back, and she could practically feel the dragon's smile as they flew back up to their floating home.

CHAPTER EIGHT

"Drink up, rearick. You look like you need it," Aysa whispered as she poured mead into Karl's large wooden mug. She patted his shoulder several times, giving it a little squeeze on the last.

Since Aysa had joined the BBB, they'd been at each other's throats, but everyone, including the two of them, knew quite well that their banter was only a reflection of a deep and abiding affection they had for each other. Karl was the father Aysa never really knew, and she was the daughter he would never have.

"Aye. Thank ye, lass. 'Twas a hell of a fight out there, wasn't it?" Karl snorted as he rolled his sore shoulder and lifted his mug with the other hand. "But we bested them arseholes like we always do."

Parker raised a glass. "To victory!"

"To victory," the rest of the fellowship responded.

"What do you think, Karl?" Hannah asked. "You want to try out one of those man-kites?"

"I'm sure I could fit a harness for you," Aysa added. "It

wouldn't have to be very big. You know, to account for the weight and all."

"No-bloody-thanks," Karl said. "I'll leave the flyin' to the damn birds."

Sal looked up from his spot in the corner and grunted.

"Dragons too, of course," Karl added. "But I like ta keep me boots on the deck, and I'd prefer it if my enemies agreed to do the same. Looking up at those flyin' bastards put a crick in me neck."

Aysa watched as Hannah stepped up behind Karl. "How about a little magical healing for you?"

"*Scheisse*, sorceress. Ye know a rearick heals faster than a bent blade of grass. But I've been around long 'nuff to know if yer offering, I'd be a damned fool to deny."

"Well, accepting doesn't mean you're *not* a damned fool, but still..." Hannah's eyes blazed red for a beat as she placed a palm on her friend's meaty shoulder and Aysa saw the pain leave his eyes. No matter how many times she saw Hannah's skills in action, they still amazed her.

"There's no shame in needing healing," Aysa said. "An old man like you has to take care of his joints."

"You keep it up, lass, and I'll give ye somethin' ta be sore over."

"What about Sal?" Vitali asked. "He looks unwell. Maybe he could use some of your healing."

Parker laughed as the dragon's stomach rumbled. "I think that's indigestion. The lizard needs more veggies in his diet, less kaffe and pirate."

Karl raised his mug. "Every man has an elixir that gives him the strength of the gods. Seems like that beast has one too." He nodded toward the kaffe vat on the serving table.

"We need to keep the little junkie moderated, though, or we might all pay fer it."

Parker rubbed a mark on his temple. "Speak for yourself. I say we hop Sal up and let him loose on any threat we find. Those pirates weren't pulling punches today. We all took our licks."

"So did the *Unlawful*," Aysa added. "I inspected her, and she is certainly beat to hell from the boarding. She's got a few more scars from the fight, but I'm not sure if it was enemy damage or the junkie dragon slamming into her. Whichever it was, I'm going to need to set her down somewhere for repairs. If I bring her back to Gregory like this, he'll kick my ass."

"Aye, girlie." Karl laughed. "Kick yer own ass. She's yer boat now. Yer the cap'n, not that nerd a thousand miles away."

Aysa nodded; Karl was right. The *Unlawful* had been built by Arcadian engineers, but she was its steward now, and she was in charge of the ship's good health. Aysa also knew that no matter how often she blamed Gregory for wanting to keep the ship in top condition, the vessel had become her baby. She wished she'd had more of an opportunity to pay back those who'd hurt her today.

She glanced at the crew, her eyes landing on Hannah who gave her an encouraging nod. "Before we all started drinking away our injuries and patting ourselves on the back for a battle well fought, I pulled out the charts Lilith left for us. The maps of this region are pretty vague. Hell, I have no idea if the people who made them were a bunch of kids doodling to burn time or explorers charting the unknown, but if the maps are right, there's a city a half a day's journey from here. I expect we should be able to set down there and mend the *Unlawful*."

"A city?" Parker exclaimed, sitting up straighter in his chair. "It feels like we haven't passed anything remotely close to civilization in months. It would be nice to get some grub that wasn't burned to death by the rearick. No offense."

"I'm only offended by yer snooty lowlander tastes," Karl added. "But I wouldn't turn down a chance to sample some local brew."

Hannah turned to Vitali. "Whatever you think."

Hannah leaned against the wall, crossed her arms, and nodded at Aysa. "I think we listen to the captain. Good job. We set sail for this city then, to right the ship and wet our whistles."

"And have some fun," Aysa said, and the Bitch and Bastard Brigade cheered right along with her.

CHAPTER NINE

The mop's water diluted the pirates' blood but didn't completely wash it away. It didn't bother Parker— much. The older burgundy stains in the wood told stories of the many foes vanquished on the *Unlawful*, and he knew there would be many more to come.

"You're pretty good with that thing," Hannah said, her voice breaking the morning silence.

He turned. The dawn sun shone on her face and made it look even more angelic than normal. There was a strange look in her eyes, something he couldn't put his finger on. Not contentment, but something adjacent to it. Maybe it was hope for something better not far beyond the horizon.

"Yeah," he finally said, leaning on the mop. "I guess it isn't much different from my spear, except for the amphorald blaster on the tip."

"Actually, I was thinking of those weeks you worked scrubbing floors at Sully's Tavern."

Parker laughed. "This pirates' blood is nothing compared to that splattered beer and puke, and gods know what else was spilled there. I lasted longer than a few weeks, didn't I?"

"Ten days, actually," Hannah said, leaning against the rail of the ship. "It took me ten whole days to convince you the work of an honest man wasn't worth it."

He nodded. "Well, you would know. You *were* kind of worthless on the streets without your leader, weren't you?"

"Excuse me?"

"You're excused." He stepped toward Hannah and wrapped his arms around her, pulling her in close. "I mean, we were on a pretty equal playing field back then."

Hannah pushed herself up on her tiptoes and gave him a long, slow kiss. Chills ran down his spine as she lingered for longer than he'd expected. They had officially been together for years, but her touch never failed to overwhelm him.

She stepped back. "Equals, huh? Believe what you want, Parker from the Boulevard, but this girl from the slums was the one who freed you from your chains."

Hannah was right, and he knew it. Although she was joking, her words held weight for him. Since they were kids pulling simple cons on the streets of Arcadia, he had always followed her lead. For Parker, there was no shame in this. It just worked. And now, after Hannah developed her skills and was juiced up by the blood of the Matriarch, he was proud to be at her side as her wingman.

"Do you miss it?" she finally asked.

"Sully's? Like an ingrown toenail."

"Arcadia. The Boulevard."

Parker stood quiet, his eyes cast out over the bow toward the land that lay before them. He could see miles of forest and trees, all coming to an end at the small mountain chain ahead. Her question struck him like none had for some time. Did he miss Arcadia? Miss his home? He really didn't know. Things had not slowed down enough to miss anything.

"I have no freaking idea," he answered. "I mean, sure. I miss aspects of it. And maybe I would miss it more if you weren't here with me."

"That's sweet."

"No," Parker said. "That's not what I mean, but I'll take boyfriend points wherever I can get them. You're my anchor to that place. When I think of Arcadia, in many ways, I think of you. You carry the best of the place with you. *We* are my memories of there. My memories of then. Sure, I miss my mother. I miss having a place. Why, are you thinking about settling down?"

Hannah shrugged. "Who wouldn't want to settle down?"

"You have a funny way of showing it, flying this ship all over Irth." Parker smiled. "Doesn't seem like settling-down behavior."

"I'm not sure," Hannah answered. "Maybe I think there's something out there for us. Someplace we can build together. You know, like Zeke tried to do with Arcadia. But maybe, just maybe, we could make it right. Make it the way it was supposed to be from the beginning without—"

"Without an Adrien stepping in and screwing the whole thing up?"

Hannah moved toward Parker and took his hand. He could feel the heat transfer between their palms. "Would it be crazy if I said yes?"

Parker interlaced his fingers with hers. "There are Adriens *everywhere*, and in every time. Hell, even Adrien wasn't Adrien when Ezekiel was building Arcadia."

"Maybe," she said. "But maybe not. Maybe we have a chance to build something real. Something whole. Maybe we find someplace that longs for redemption. Maybe there's a city out there big enough for us."

The morning light shifted as the *Unlawful* crested the hill-line.

"Like that?" Parker said, pointing across the bow toward a city on the horizon that was bigger than any he had ever seen.

CHAPTER TEN

Although the dusty earth between Vitali's toes sent a sense of comfort through his body, his feet weren't used to this land. His place back in Kaskara was a jungle. The tough soles were accustomed to the squish of moss and the slop of marshy forests. But still, his people had stayed low to the ground for a reason. Even with his feline propensities, he preferred the low-hanging trees of the forest.

"Good thing I grabbed this from Super Nerd before we headed out," Aysa said, waving a little black box in her hand just after hitting the ground behind him. "I, for one, am ready to go sow some oats."

Aysa was one of his favorite members of the team. Hell, she was nearly everyone's favorite, even if she volleyed insults at them, especially the men, with more practice than the rocks she lobbed from her oversized hand. The Baseeki girl was like everyone's little sister, and Vitali had been taken by her as well.

"Sow some oats?"

"Yeah. You know, have some fun. I insist on having fun wherever I am." She looked around the circle and then up the rope ladder they had just descended. Everyone was on the ground except for Karl, who was struggling down the rope ladder. "It's easy to have fun with the Bitch and Bastard Brigade. Like this."

Aysa grabbed the tail end of the ladder and whipped it, the wave hitting Karl on the legs. He squinted down at her, red-faced.

"Aye," she yelled in her best Karl impersonation. "Move yer arse, rearick!"

She held the remote up, and Karl's eyes got enormous. "Doncha dare, ye little pipsqueak."

"No time to spare." Aysa flicked the switch, and the amphorald core on the ship hummed as the vessel edged skyward.

"*Scheisse!*" Karl screamed from twenty feet overhead.

The rearick let go of the rope, and Vitali froze as the little man's body plunged toward the dusty earth. Just before hitting the deck, he froze in place, hovered for a second, and then lightly drifted to his feet.

"Ye mangy, long-armed, sweaty piece of pubescent scum. Ye coulda killed me!" he screamed, stomping toward Aysa.

Looking over his shoulder, Vitali saw Hannah's eyes shift from red to their normal color. "I've got your back, rearick." She laughed.

"Ye shouldn't hafta, Hannah. And what if ye weren't—"

Aysa dropped to the ground, laughing. "See, Vitali? We have fun *everywhere*." She stood and skipped over to Karl. "Come on, short stuff. I knew she had you."

Karl's face turned blaze-red. "One of these days, Aysa. One of these days."

"What?" she asked. "You're gonna ask me out on a proper date? I can't wait."

"All right, you two finished?" Hannah said.

"I haven't even begun to deal with this 'un," Karl spat.

"Come on, Karl," Hannah shot back. "It *was* pretty funny. Anyway, we need to roll. We have no idea what this place will hold, and it will be good to get inside the city walls before the sun goes down. We haven't seen much in the way of civilization for many miles, so who knows how often these people get visitors?"

"Let's move," Vitali said, hoping that a good march would calm the rearick down.

He took the lead, with Parker by his side. The two of them had become close since Vitali had joined the team. Even with their differences, they were quite similar, not only in their fighting styles but also in their dispositions.

After nearly a half-hour of walking in silence, Parker finally noted, "It's pretty dead out here."

"Dead quiet," Vitali agreed. "I mean, Hannah was right. There wasn't much in the way of towns or even small hamlets lying off the border of the city, but there were plenty of farms. You would think that there'd be at least *some* farmers transporting their goods on this road or traveling back home after a normal day of trading."

Parker nodded, his eyes scanning the horizon. "You would think that, wouldn't you? Then again, I don't remember the last time I arrived in a town where everything was normal. Hell, I have no idea what normal even is anymore."

Vitali laughed. "Pretty sure we have been born into abnormal times, my friend. But maybe someday we'll find a place that is good old-fashioned boring."

Parker smiled. "Or make one."

Vitali let Parker's words drift between them. He knew enough about their hometown, Arcadia, and what had become of it. Over the months together, he had heard the stories of the slum Parker and Hannah had grown up in and the way they had fought to overcome the oppressive regent who ruled the city. He also knew the town was supposed to have been normal, or at least, that was what Ezekiel had intended when he laid its cornerstone so many years before.

"Am I interrupting something?" Hannah asked as she joined them.

"Just guy talk," Parker said. "You know, big fights, hot women, cold ale."

Hannah laughed. "Yeah. I'm glad my boyfriend isn't a typical guy."

Parker shrugged. "As long as I'm with you, I'm always with a hot woman and in the middle of a big fight."

"And the ale?"

"That's what Karl's for," Parker replied.

"Well, I don't want to break up the bro-fest, but we're coming up on the city."

Vitali nodded, his eyes on the walls. "You and Parker take point. I'll bring up the rear. It's the way to go."

Hannah forced a smile. He knew that she knew exactly what was going through Vitali's brain. When you want to make friends amongst the humans, you don't lead with the kitty-cat. It was common sense. He didn't need her sympathy.

Ever since he'd left his homeland he'd learned to navigate this new world of being a freak everywhere he turned. Sure, Aysa had long-ass arms and Karl was the height of an overgrown kid, but they were nothing compared to the guy covered in fur who sported a tail and cat eyes.

"Yeah. And sorry—"

He held up a hand. "No need, Hannah. This is strategy, plain and simple. I also pretty distinctly remember the first time you and I met."

Hannah smiled. "You were scary as hell, but it wasn't just the way you looked. It was the thought of having to fight you."

"Good thing we never exchanged blows," Vitali said. "Pretty sure you would be using my hide for a throw rug in front of the fire on the *Unlawful*."

"Slippers," Hannah replied. "I had a nice pair of slippers in mind, but I prefer orange."

"Oooh, I want some cat slippers!" Aysa cooed.

"I have a cousin you could fight. She's a pretty deep orange, with some flecks of blonde. Would make a good pair of cat slippers, and to be quite honest, I don't think most of the family would miss her during the holidays," Vitali said.

Sal looked over his shoulder at him, tongue shooting in and out.

"Hang out in back with me, Sal." Vitali gave him a nod. "We freaks will stick together."

The Brigade marched on in silence toward the city gate. While the others looked forward to nothing but a little rest and relaxation, Vitali didn't feel quite so comforted by the foreign stronghold before him. Other than the empty roads leading toward the gate, there was something not quite right about the place.

He'd seen scores of cities outside of his homeland and every single one of them gave him the creeps. In his gut, he knew it was because off his native soil, he was, and would remain, an oddity at best. At worst, he was an aberration whom furless bipeds would be pleased to string up on the city walls by a noose or find a spike on which to fasten his head. Few were as accepting as Hannah the magician and her band of misfits.

Twenty yards farther along, the city guards came into sight. There was absolutely nothing extraordinary about them, just a few common men putting in a day's work. As the Brigade halved the distance between them, the men stood at attention, making themselves look almost intimidating enough to scare off a remnant child.

When they were five yards away, the one on the left raised a hand motioning for them to stop.

"State your business in Solyr," he growled with all the hospitality of a mother bear defending her cubs.

Hannah stepped ahead of the group. "I am Hannah of Arcadia. We travel from New Romanov on an adventure to chart these lands and the lands to the south. Yesterday, we ran into pirates who tried their damnedest to take our vehicle. They've been dealt with, but we come to you for a bit of respite from the road and supplies to repair her."

The men exchanged glances and then looked back at Hannah. "And the rest of your group? Are they back with the craft?"

Hannah grinned. "We *are* the crew, friend. Now, can we enter your city?"

The men looked exchanged glances and spoke in low tones. Finally, the other shouted back to them, "Impossible! We know the pirates of the region well. They take what they want, and those journeying through the land if they are wise, give them what they ask. The foolish end up dead, or slaves. Four people, a beast, and whatever that is," he pointed at Vitali, "could not best the pirates hereabouts. The farmers of this region pay a good percentage to keep them at bay."

Hannah glanced at Parker, who gave her a slight shake of the head.

"Well, I guess we're better with swords than your common farmer, then. We mean no ill. Will you give us—and our coin—passage into the city, or should we be on our way?"

The men conferred again, and then took two steps apart from one another. "You may pass, but if you have come to do harm, you will find our swords have a harsher bite than the pirates', and our wills are stronger than the west wind."

"Aye, that's some ripe bullshite if ye ask me," Karl murmured under his breath. Vitali watched Aysa jab him in the ribs. "What? They look like their wills are no stronger than the wind comin' outta me arse."

"Thank you, sirs," Hannah replied loudly. "You will find we mean no ill to your good city."

Hannah led the way between the men. They stood at attention and raised their arms as Sal sauntered past them, taking a second to stare each man up and down as if he were a medium-rare steak. They exhaled once the dragon had passed them, and then their eyes locked on Vitali. He was expecting shock or awe, and he wouldn't have blamed them. In most human eyes, he was some kind of freak, like a man dressed in a costume on stage for the circus, but these guards didn't look surprised. They looked worried. Like they had dealt with his kind before and had come away lesser for it.

That's impossible, he thought. *We're thousands of miles from Kaskara.*

Passing through the gates, Vitali expected the place to be alive with activity. He hoped to become invisible in the crowded streets and marketplaces. Instead, the crew was met by near-silence. The promenade from the gate to the center of the town was almost empty. Only a few pedestrians were on the brick pathway, all of them scurrying with their heads down.

Karl grunted. "Aye, not the party I was expecting fer a few days off the damned boat."

"Yeah," Parker agreed. "Something's off. Kind of reminds me of—"

"When Adrien really turned the screws on Arcadia?"

"Exactly," Parker answered. "Only then the Guard would be on the streets. Nobles. But this is just plain eerie."

They walked on, each of the warriors on high alert. Vitali's senses were tuned in, his keen sense of smell and hearing searching for anything out of the ordinary. But there was nothing out of the ordinary. Nothing at all, which was, in and of itself, a little weird. In a city of this size, there was always something to set off his senses.

Rows of buildings rose around him, and although he

was used to the hulking canopy of the rainforest, the buildings made him feel claustrophobic. He kept glancing over his shoulder and up at the rooftops, waiting for some kind of evil to attack, like a leopard from the thick growth of his homeland.

But there was nothing. Absolutely nothing, and "nothing" was more unnerving than an onslaught of a dozen Muur warriors. To his relief, the towering buildings grew shorter and more austere as they pushed farther into the town and found its center. When he caught up with the BBB, each of its members was standing still, staring up at a statue taller than all the structures they had passed.

"*Scheisse*, lass," Karl whispered in reverence. "Seemed they knew ye were comin'. They built a damned statue in yer honor."

As far as Vitali could tell, the rearick was right. Standing before them was an image of a woman artfully carved from marbled stone. Her jaw was set, ready for war, and her eyes, made of red gemstones, bore down on them. Every feature of the woman was perfect from her jawline to her brow. The only difference from Hannah was that the statue held a weapon at the ready, a long sword built for two hands—one like the ancients of his region had used. It was said the people before the Madness had called it a katana.

Hannah stared at the statue. After what seemed like a fortnight, she finally spoke. "If only I could be like that."

"Hell, yeah," Aysa said. "She's freaking *huge*. Who is she, a blood relative of yours?"

Hannah shook her head. "In a way. That's the Matriarch. That's Bethany Anne."

Vitali stared up at the statue in wonder. Everywhere they went, they heard legends of the Queen Bitch, who'd saved the world and kept it safe by taking her fight against evil among the stars. He knew Hannah carried more than her blood in her veins; she carried the Matriarch's mission. It was what drove the young woman to protect Irth and kept her vigilant against the darkness.

Vitali couldn't help but wonder if it was too big a burden to bear, even for someone as strong as Hannah, but if he had a stack of chips to bet, he'd put them all on her. In all his days, he'd met no one stronger or smarter in battle.

Their moment of silent homage to the Queen didn't last long. Shouts broke through the quiet, empty square. First came a few voices, clearly volleying words at one another, and slowly, many others joined the chorus.

The team stood, their eyes shifting from the ancient, powerful figure immortalized in stone to the powerful one of flesh in their midst.

"Looks like we have some work to do," Hannah remarked.

"I'll be dipped in hog shite. We been on that boat fer weeks, and me lips just want a touch of ale." Karl's knuckles whitened as his calloused hand gripped his hammer. "I thought we came here fer a little fun."

Aysa pulled her shield from her back and strapped it onto her arm. "Come on, rearick! This *is* fun."

She took off toward the sounds of violence with Hannah at her side. Vitali's heart rate increased, and he could feel the hair down the center of his back stand up. As the crew turned a corner, the city opened into a park two blocks wide by two blocks long. Simple benches and play structures had been placed in perfectly designed patterns. The city had certainly had leisure in mind when they created the space.

But today, the park was anything but playful.

Team BBB arrived just as the first punches were thrown, and before they could step across the road and into the fray, an all-out brawl ensued. Men and women and even a few teens cursed and kicked and punched. In the midst of it all were a few bursts of flame and even a shock of electricity.

Magic users, Vitali thought. That meant trouble.

"We've gotta help," Hannah said.

"Yeah," Vitali answered, his eyes scanning the crowd. "But help who?"

Hannah's eyes flashed red for a beat, then she shook her head. "I have no idea. I've tried to read them, but all I am getting is fear and anger. Let's do our best to just break them up, so use restraint." She pointed at Aysa, who was unfurling her bolas, letting them swing like the weights of an old grandfather clock. "Especially you."

"Me?" she asked with a smile and a raised eyebrow.

"For Irth!" Parker yelled.

"For the Matriarch!" Hannah cried, and the crew pushed into the dusty melee.

CHAPTER ELEVEN

Hannah had been in hundreds of fights since Ezekiel asked her to join his quest, and before that, Hannah had spent years navigating the frenzy of a large city at war with itself. While her experience helped her keep her cool and gave her the skills she needed to assess a situation like this, it gave no advice as to how to proceed.

There were clearly two factions at war here: a group of physical magic users who seemed fairly adept at basic fighting skills and another group that seemed...strange. They possessed no outward form of spellcraft, yet they moved with a speed and strength that showed the obvious presence of nanocytes in their blood. These two forces crashed into one another like thunderclouds, and Hannah knew that if she did nothing, it would soon rain blood.

So she did something.

Two women, eyes glowing yellow, with large black spikes growing out of their forearms, were whaling on a man in expensive-looking green clothing. Hannah ran to help him, grabbing the spiky women by the shoulders and throwing them aside. A man with a thick growth on his head like horns charged at her, and she caught him by the spikes, and with a gentle twist, sent him sprawling. These body-magic users had some strength behind them, and they knew how to use it, but Hannah had strength as well. A young man, shorter than Karl but with huge arms, took a swing at her. Hannah stepped aside easily, knocking him to the ground with the back of her hand.

But if her strength helped her fight, it didn't win her any favors from the other side. Two women with glossy black eyes pushed their hands forward and shot angry-looking shafts of light in her direction. Hannah lifted her arms, pulling a wall of dirt and cobblestone up to shield her, and with a flick of her wrist, she shot the wall in their direction, bowling them both over. The attack reminded her of a move she'd seen Ezekiel use once, and she knelt, forcing her magic outward in concentric circles. The ground began to soften, and before long, the mob was slogging through a foot of thick mud.

That should slow them down, she thought. And it did. But it also gave every pissed-off person there a perfect target. Angry voices filled the air.

"Myrna scum!"

"Burn the Mylek witch!"

Within seconds, the mob had turned on her. She could hear Parker and Karl shouting, but without turning their weapons on the crowd, they couldn't get to her. Hannah was alone, dodging gnarled club-like hands and magic spells alike. It took a surprising amount of effort to go easy on them, but Hannah hadn't come to this city to spill blood.

"I just...wanted...a damn...drink!" she shouted while lifting a woman with skin like stone over her head.

As she tossed her quarry back into the crowd, Hannah spotted a young woman—she couldn't have been older than twenty—going toe-to-toe with a half-dozen magic users. The girl moved fast, her footwork elegant and smooth like a dancer's, and when she landed a fist, she saw bodies crumple. Her body magic was powerful, but the numbers were against her. She took a magical bolt to the back, then another, and the well-dressed magicians moved in for the kill.

But Hannah had other things in mind. She teleported into their midst, and the force of her sudden arrival from nowhere knocked them on their asses. They took one look at Hannah's red-eyed fury and ran.

She turned back to the girl, who stared at her in wonder.

"Who the hell are you?" she asked.

"I'm Hannah. You okay?"

Before the girl could answer, a clear trumpet note, high and angry, rang out over the crowd. Hannah looked up to find the source, and when she turned back, the girl was gone.

Whatever the trumpet signified, the crowd all got the message. They scattered from the scene, dragging their injured along with them. Seconds later, the BBB was alone in the town square.

"So much fer rest and relaxation," Karl muttered.

"Don't give up hope," Parker said. "It looks like a welcome party has just arrived."

As he spoke, Hannah could see the column of soldiers

entering the square. They were dressed like the guards at the front gate, and they carried mean metal clubs.

"What's the meaning of this?" a large man at the front shouted. He had a bushy mustache that reminded Hannah of Laurel's squirrel Devin.

"My name is Hannah, and we're—"

Mr. Mustache wasn't in a listening mood. "Throw them in irons. We'll settle this at the keep."

The soldiers spread out and placed a hand on Aysa's shoulder. She broke the hand.

"Any of you bastards try to put me in chains, I'll bust your knees in."

"Enough, Aysa!" Hannah shouted. The angry Baseeki looked at her questioningly. "It's okay, trust me. Everyone, let's just do what they say."

Hannah stepped forward, her arms in front of her. The commander grabbed a pair of shackles and locked them together. "By order of the Kingdom of Solyr, you all are under arrest.

CHAPTER TWELVE

T he only thing that chapped a rearick's ass more than allowing himself to be put into chains was seeing another man hold his hammer. At the moment, Karl was dealing with both of those ass-chapping situations. The rusty links, clearly made for someone of a taller stature, dragged between his legs, threatening to catch every raised cobblestone in the city street, but Karl's eyes remained fixed on the soldier with the rearick's hammer resting on his shoulder.

His trust in Hannah was the only thing keeping Karl from wrapping his shackles around the man's neck and squeezing the life from him. Their leader had grown, not only in her magic and ability to throw a mean right hook, but also in her wisdom. The girl from the Boulevard had been replaced by a shrewd strategist, and Karl had every intention of following her lead.

The image of saving her from a wild boar in the woods outside Arcadia years ago was still seared in his mind.

Hannah was only a shadow of that kid now, and he would walk in her shadow to the brink of death if she asked him.

After a few minutes of stewing, Karl forced himself to shift his attention from his ire to gathering intel. If he knew anything, it was that his bondage would not last. He expected that anything he could learn about the city would be nothing but helpful, since this little stopover had turned into an adventure in its own right.

The city, although larger, was much like Arcadia. As they passed between buildings that rose three and four stories overhead, he could tell it wasn't a restored stronghold from the days before the Madness. The large rocks had been hewn in the same fashion as those in Arcadia, stone by stone, by magic users.

Stores lined their path: a grocery, a cobbler, and a smithy marked by a sign in the shape of an anvil. In many ways, it was a place like any other that had learned to thrive in the lowlands among remnant and marauders. The only difference between Solyr and a handful of other cities they had visited on their journey around Irth was that this place was *dead*.

The windows of the stores were shuttered. The streets were empty. Occasional eyes peering out between thick, drawn blinds were the only signs of life, except for the guards marching them toward gods knew where. The desolate streets, paired with the mob brawl in the park, told him one thing: something in this prosperous town had gone sideways. The shit had hit the fan, and Karl and his friends had walked in downwind.

Looking between the rows of soldiers leading the way, Karl saw their destination. Dark stone piled upon dark stone. Bars on the windows and a giant oak door. He'd seen a hundred buildings like it in a hundred different cities. He'd spent more than his fair share of nights inside their walls. They'd landed, wanting nothing more than some supplies for the *Unlawful*, a solid meal and drink, and a soft bed. Now it was clear they would be sleeping on a jail-cell cot if this city was kind to their prisoners.

Just before the steps leading up to the prison, the captain of the guard stopped and turned to face his men and the prisoners. His face, stern in the middle of the park, had changed. His features looked less like the hard-ass captain and more like a kid who'd just awoken from a deep sleep.

"Plans have changed," he said to his men. "We're going to the great hall."

A thin smile spread under Karl's beard as he glanced up at Hannah.

Her eyes were white. She had influenced his mind.

Sometimes, I love them freakin' wizards, he thought.

CHAPTER THIRTEEN

The enormous double doors opened into a giant room with vaulted ceilings. Three guards and the captain stepped in first. Parker and his friends were shoved across the threshold behind them. He couldn't help but grin like a fool. He had no idea what Hannah was cooking up, but she had already saved them from a night in a foreign cell. If things kept going this way, they'd be granted the key to the city before sunset.

His eyes scanned the room, first taking in the exits that sat on either side of a large, empty throne. The doors had knobs and locks. He had no idea if they could make a quick escape that way. Windows stretching from floor to ceiling made the room bright with natural light, and it felt bigger than its already gargantuan size. They also provided a way out if things came to that. He pulled the chains holding his wrists apart once more, wondering if they might exhibit any sort of weakness. Just like before, they held firm. But Parker knew he had someone stronger than iron on his team. It just so happened that he shared a room with her at the end of the day.

Besides the guards, there were twelve people around a giant oval table, each of them filling out an overstuffed chair. At the head stood a man about Parker's height. His clothes were a nicer version of those of the magic users they had fought in the park. Parker knew this man, like the others in the room, had considerable resources.

The well-dressed folk didn't notice the entrance of the captors and guards. They were too busy taking turns shouting at one another.

"We would be damned fools if we didn't divert all cash reserves toward security, especially in a time like this. If we don't mend the holes in our already weakened defenses, we will have to endure more of the same. Attack from without, treachery from within," the man standing at the head of the table said.

A woman, whose strong, angular features contrasted with her slender form, stood. It was hard to tell under her billowing dress, but he guessed she was related to the warriors going toe-to-toe with the magic users in the park —a position she mirrored here. Her eyes were locked on the angry man at the head of the table. "There is treachery within, Kirill. You and I agree on that. But that is precisely where our agreement ends. What good are strong walls if the people protected within starve? Do we need defenses? Yes. Every city does. But the Guard is able; they just need stronger leadership."

Parker's eyes shifted to the captain, who grimaced at her remark, fists balled tightly at his sides. Parker could tell the man was doing all he could to keep his composure under the attack.

The man named Kirill laughed at her. "Ky, it is always the same for you. If Solyr provided each of her citizens with a bag of barley and three fattened calves a week, you would bang the same drum." He glanced at the men on his right and left, and they nodded their approval. "*The poor, the poor,*" he whined in a high singsong. "If the people are hungry, they should work harder."

"But my people—" the woman named Ky began.

Kirill raised a hand. "They are *all our* people, Ky. Must you divide us at every breath? My father would have had none of this."

"Your father's body is barely cold, and already you insist on twisting his words and misinterpreting his intentions."

"He was a good man," Kirill spat. "Far better than anyone here."

Ky smiled. "You might be more right about that than you let on. King Aurel was certainly better than the bastard who is attempting to sit on his throne." She pointed at the jewel-encrusted seat at the end of the room. "And the Mylek won't let you steal from us what is not yet rightfully yours. We will die first."

"Then die, you must!" the man next to Kirill shouted.

The words threw the room into a frenzy. Parties on both sides began to shout and wag their fingers at one another indiscriminately. None were safe, and none were silent.

"Sir," the captain of the guard called over the bedlam. Kirill didn't hear him. "*Sir,*" he yelled.

Finally, Kirill looked up from the red-faced crowd and

saw his captain of the guard, his troops, and a group of strangers shackled before him.

Kirill's face twisted in confusion. "Silence!" He stepped around the table and approached them. Ky walked double-time on his heels. "What the hell is this, Irmand?" Kirill asked. He looked down at the chained Sal, who was wagging his tail. To Parker, the dragon looked no more ferocious than a dog on a leash, but there was no telling how the big lizard made these people feel. The man's eyes widened when they landed on Vitali.

"My Lord, we caught these outsiders making trouble in the town square. They say that they're only here to fix their vessel and continue their voyage, but my troops pulled them out of a violent brawl. For all we know, they started it."

Parker could see the flush rising in Karl's cheeks, and he placed his hand on his friend's shoulder, more as a symbol than anything. The rearick's muscles were tight and he was ready for action.

"But why the hell did you bring them to us?" Ky asked. "Can't you see we're in the middle of deliberation? A heated one, at that. Take care of the foreigners yourself. That is what we pay you for, after all." She pursed her lips and kept her gaze on Irmand, the captain of the guard.

He looked back at her blankly, as if he were trying to process exactly what she had said.

"Irmand?" Ky asked again. "What is wrong with you?"

Irmand turned toward his troops, and then looked at his captives one at a time. Parker bit inside of his cheek to keep from laughing. He had seen people in this predicament many times before, but it still got him every time.

The woman walked up to Team BBB, eyeing them. Then she turned to Irmand. "My gods, the captain of the guard has been bewitched."

"I-I..." Irmand stammered, which brought a tremendous laugh from Kirill.

"It is true, my friend. For the first time all day, I will admit this: Ky is correct about something." He turned toward the others still seated around the table. "And this," he waved his hand toward Parker and his friends, "proves my point. This ragtag group is Exhibit A. Do we not need stronger defenses? Are we strong enough to protect against the enemy outside our gates? Our walls high enough, and our men strong enough? I think the answer to that question lies right before you, dear Ky."

He turned and walked back toward the table, leaving the captives behind. Before he reached his seat at the end of the table, Ky started to clap, and the slow, rhythmic sound echoed through the chamber. "Very well played, Kirill. Where did you get them?" She nodded toward Hannah's crew. "Certainly, it took some work to get a group of foreign mages, even one this small, to come take part in your clever ruse."

Kirill reached his spot and slammed his giant palms on the oak table. "And if an army of a thousand remnant or the pirates from the north invaded, would they also be called my charge? Not everything is a false flag, my dear." His tone went higher, and a vein popped out on the side of his neck. He stood tall. "I will not allow my father's legacy to fall for the sake of breadcrumbs for your little urchins throughout the city. I will not let the good people of Solyr suffer at the hands of those outside these walls because your heart bleeds for people who cannot help themselves. My family has worked too hard. Too long. I will do what it takes to stop you and—"

"Enough," Hannah yelled. As she did, she lifted her hands, eyes blazing red, and pulled her chains apart. They didn't just break; the iron disintegrated and fell as dust at her feet. Swords were drawn and the troops stepped toward her, but they stopped when they saw what came next.

Hannah put her hands out toward the walls as her body started to levitate to the vaulted ceiling. She crossed her hands over her chest in an intricate pattern and then extended them above her shoulders toward the rafters. Wind whipped around her, lifting and tossing her hair like snakes on ancient Medusa. Lightning crackled from her fingertips. She turned her hand toward the table.

Both sides quivered and trembled in fear. It was Ky who pointed and shouted, "The Matriarch!"

The guards dropped to a knee as the politicians continued to tremble. Hannah flicked her wrist toward her crew, and their chains disintegrated, just as hers had. Parker, Aysa, and Vitali moved to cover the guards, and Karl grabbed his hammer, which was resting on the stone floor.

Hannah drifted back down and landed squarely in the center of the table. All eyes were on her.

"Will one of you tell me what the hell is going on here?"

CHAPTER FOURTEEN

Hannah followed Kirill and Ky into an adjacent room. Her crew was right behind her, the Guard and Irmand behind them. Apparently, the two elders wanted to have this conversation without the rest of the group present, but they were afraid to be alone without their soldiers' protection. Hannah had no idea why, and she wasn't sure if it should bring her comfort or concern her. What she did know was that this group would be no match for the Bitch and Bastard Brigade.

They entered a room that, in comparison to the throne room, was what one might consider cozy. The ceiling was much lower, only about ten feet. Instead of the enormous table and chairs, there was a circle of furniture made from what looked to be exotic leather. Nothing was spared in the house of the king.

Kirill motioned to a large couch and a wingback chair, and Hannah and her crew took their places. It wasn't until they were in their seats that Kirill and Ky sat. Irmand and his men remained at the door, weapons in hand.

"We will tell you what's going on here," Kirill said. "But first, I want to know about you. Who are you, and what are you *really* doing here? And before you answer, you should know that I have a gift of sniffing out lies."

"And dishing them out," Ky quipped. Kirill shot her a glare.

Hannah nodded. "Fair enough. My friends and I have traveled from New Romanov, a city many days' travel from here to the north." She looked at each of them to see if their faces showed any recognition of the name, which they didn't. "Frankly, we're just exploring. None of the people in the city have traveled very far south. I guess you could say adventure is in our blood, but we're not marauders. Not troublemakers. We're just on our way to discover new lands, or at least we were until we got boarded."

Ky raised an eyebrow. "Boarded?"

"Yes. We have a ship. Not one that sails, one that flies." Kirill's eyes widened. "It's a technology built by a comingling of the tech of the new world and the old in a city far away from here. In Arcadia, my city. When we were less than a day's travel north of here, our ship was boarded by pirates, a group of real asshats who thought they could make a little scratch taking our ship. And maybe us."

"Let's just say those guys didn't go home to see their mommies," Aysa added.

"I've heard of those pirates," Kirill said, ignoring Aysa. "They have ventured toward us before, but thankfully we've been able to fend them off. Our walls are a major defense," he glanced at Ky, "but unfortunately, I'm not sure the defenses will last through a major attack."

Hannah smiled. "Yeah. I heard most of that conversation a couple of minutes ago. Seems like you two need couples counseling. Anyway, we didn't come here to start trouble. We didn't come to your town to solve problems either. We just happened to wander into the royal rumble that was taking place in your town square. Apparently, you've got some issues on your hands."

"And what business is that of yours?" Irmand, the captain of the guard, shouted, but Kirill waved him down.

"Let's just say that solving issues is kind of our forte," Hannah said. "But if you all want to tear yourselves apart, I guess that is *your* business."

Kirill nodded slowly and waited. Hannah knew he was measuring his response. Whoever this guy was, he was careful. Smart. Shrewd, even.

Before he could respond, Ky jumped in. "You could say we have a significant amount of unrest, but this is new to us. Overall, the people of Solyr are peace-loving."

She paused, which gave Kirill a chance to speak. "This unrest is what happens when power shifts in any city. There are those who want to subvert the group in control and question the authority of leadership. We have people who want to deny the rightful claim of tradition."

Hannah used her mental magic to infiltrate Kirill's mind.

This city is my responsibility now. This city is my responsibility now. This city is my responsibility now.

The phrase repeated in his mind, and Hannah wondered if it was some kind of prayer. He seemed concerned about his place and his people. Hannah scratched an itch forming behind her ears and tried to focus on the conversation happening around her.

"Kirill is correct," Ky said. "There *has* been a shift in power. The city's beloved King Aurel suffered a terrible death. The tradition of Solyr is that the kingdom is handed down to a successor based upon the king's proclamation, but King Aurel left no such direction for his city. That is why his son," Ky glanced Kirill, "is trying to gain control by certain machinations."

Kirill shook his head. "Your mouth is full of half-truths, Ky, as it has been since your birth." He leveled his eyes on Hannah, his face swept with emotion. "It is true. My father is dead, and perhaps he considered himself to be more than mortal, like the rest of us. He never named his successor, but most would agree on his intent. I served by his side for decades, from my youth until his death. In keeping with tradition, I affirm the compact of our city that if no successor has been named, then the people will cast their votes for the one who will lead them into the future. For us, only when the monarchy stutters does democracy step in. This is our way."

"Okay," Parker said. "Then why not just hold a vote?"

"It's not that simple," Ky said, shaking her head. "The good king did not just die, he was murdered. How can we trust the people to vote honestly when the truth is hidden from them?"

Kirill nodded, his face like granite. "We agree on more than I expected this day, Ky. It is true that the assassins *must* be found and they also will be dealt with extremely judiciously. But that shouldn't interrupt the rule of law, no matter this chaos provides certain...political advantages for a particular group."

"And what exactly are you accusing me of?" Ky's eyes narrowed. "I loved Aurel, same as you."

"I'm just saying that the Mylek have the most to gain from succession through a ballot. My father's untimely demise has cracked open a door for you."

Ky opened her mouth to say something but held it in. As the woman's emotions rose, Hannah took the opportunity to dip into her mind. Unlike Kirill, Ky's thoughts were tumultuous and filled with rage. It seemed that it wasn't unusual for people like Kirill, the Myrna, to lay blame on the Mylek people. Every city had a story, and Hannah was starting to understand pieces of theirs.

"Be cautious," Ky continued, her eyes faintly yellow. "One shouldn't insult a Mylek lightly."

"A Myrna never does," Kirill said. He turned back toward Hannah. "As you can see, things aren't great at the moment, and the tension rests on more than me and dear Ky here. These damned Blue Scarves, for example, have been making trouble every chance they get."

"Blue scarves?"

Irmand broke in from across the room. "The Blue Scarves are nothing but a gnat on the ass of an ox. Trouble-makers with little power and fewer wits, trying to cause disarray on our streets. My men will—"

Ky cleared her throat. "These *gnats* are on *your* ass, Irmand, and it seems that your men have done precious little to keep their random acts of chaos at bay. Your Guard is weak, and they lack discipline. With the election coming, I recommend you tighten up your ship. A good portion of our wealth goes to arming you and your men, but still, you can hardly keep them under your watch. More and more of your men are deserting their posts."

"Irmand is doing what he can," Kirill said. "The city is splitting at the seams. If we do not act now, we might not have any sort of union by the time of the election."

Hannah stood. "Okay, so the king is dead, and all hell is breaking out, with some douche nuggets causing problems on the streets, a murderer on the loose, and a city guard that can't keep its men in the ranks." She looked at her crew.

"Nothin' we haven't handled before," Karl croaked.

"Indeed. If you will have us, the Bitch and Bastard Brigade is here to help."

Ky looked up at her, her eyes full of doubt. "I don't understand. Why would you do this? Why would you help us?"

Hannah thought for a second. She considered using her mental magic to make the point but decided a forthright answer would do the trick just as well.

"We've traveled all over Irth, and we've seen more than our fair share of chaos and bloodshed. Everywhere we go, civilization barely holds on, clinging to what little it has." She looked around the room. "I don't know your city, but I've known others like it. You might have troubles, but you also have thousands of innocent people who trust your laws and those walls. I can't just sit back and watch the peace you've made here be torn apart, not if I can help."

She gazed at her team, the finest group of warriors and heroes she'd ever known. She could tell that they were with her one hundred percent.

"You've seen but a fraction of what my team can do,"

Hannah continued, "and that was enough for half your council to bow down and worship me as the Matriarch. I'm sorry to say I'm not her. If she were here, she could solve the issue with a flick of her sword. I might not be the Matriarch, but the truth is, I've got her blood in my veins, and if I can use that power to heal your city, then by the gods, I will do it."

CHAPTER FIFTEEN

Vitali walked through the ornately decorated hallway, hoping to outpace the screams behind him. But the great hall was large, and he was still a little uneasy navigating indoors.

He turned a corner and found a statue he recognized.

Kirill had set the BBB up in guest quarters. It was no hammock under the peaceful boughs of trees, but it beat sleeping in the cramped rooms on the *Unlawful*. Two more turns brought him to the open door to the common room, where the rest of the crew had gathered except for Hannah. He stepped through it, heart still racing, and took a seat at the edge of the room.

Sal looked up at him before curling back up into a tight, scaly ball for a nap.

"You okay, Fuzztastick?" Aysa asked with a grin.

Vitali lied, "Fine."

Aysa jumped off her round chair and put her face close to his. Her large eyes narrowed like she was trying to read his mind. "I don't buy it. What happened?"

Vitali sighed. "While you all were settling in, I decided to have a look around the grand hall. The artwork in this strange land is amazing, and I guess I got lost in the sights. It turns out, however, that the people who live here are less impressed by the sight that I make. A small child thought I was a monster who had come to devour her."

"I bet she was a Myrna," Parker said. "They seem to have a bias against people who don't quite look like people."

Karl sat on a couch large enough to make him look like a child. He raised his mug toward Vitali. "Aye, it's bad enough around here to be built fer the caves. Me stature makes me a freak too. Can't imagine if ye covered me with fur and gave me one of them tails of yers."

Aysa wrinkled her nose and pointed at Karl's long beard. "*If* you were covered with fur?"

"Shut it, Long Arms."

Before Aysa had a chance to shoot back her retort, bells rang from a tower somewhere in the city. After three chimes, the door flew open, and Hannah filled the space. Sal jumped to his feet and ran toward her.

"Nice entrance, babe," Parker said to her.

"Aysa isn't the only one with a flair for the dramatic. But the bells do not toll for me. I was told by Kirill that for years, those bells have been reserved for the beginning of city festivals," she said.

"And what are they there for now?" Vitali asked.

"To warn of danger." Hannah looked at her team. "Grab your gear, everybody. It's go time."

The three other members filed out of the room, each of them ready to get to work. Vitali sat still in his chair. He hoped Hannah would just move on, that she and his others wouldn't notice he was missing. Deep down, he knew that was an impossibility.

"What's up, V?"

"I'm going to sit this one out, Captain."

Hannah's eyes narrowed, not out of anger but confusion. They had fought side by side more times than either of them could remember, and Vitali never sat out a fight. "Is there something I need to know?"

Vitali stood and pushed his shoulders back. The Lynqi were nothing if not proud. He wouldn't defame his people's name in front of the most powerful magician in the world. He could only hope she would understand.

"I'm not sure I belong."

Hannah laughed. "Have you been listening to these jokers? I don't think *any* of us belong here. Especially not Aysa, but we're all still trying to figure out where the Baseeki actually belong. That's why we're perfect together. We're all a bunch of misfits. Just look at Sal."

Vitali laughed. "Everyone loves Sal. Everyone. But some misfits fit less than others."

He told her what happened with the young girl, and Hannah's face transformed as she listened. She had the power of the gods in her control, but she also had a warmth of heart that could melt the Frozen North. Growing up in the Boulevard had nurtured a sense of empathy in her that was its own superpower.

"You don't need to hide from these people."

"I'm not hiding," he said. "I'm helping. This city is fit to explode, and our job is to calm it down. We can't do that if people freak out at the sight of me. Let me stay behind, and I'll do what I'm good at."

"You're good at fighting," Hannah said.

Vitali laughed. "We're all good at fighting. Each and every one of us is good at other things, too. Aysa can build, Karl can command, Parker can con. But me, I can smell a rat. Something didn't strike me right about the story of good King Aurel. Let me stay and do some recon. Like our ancient brothers the cats, Lynqi like me know how to disappear or blend into the background when we need to. If I stick around here, I might just be able to come up with something useful, maybe even crucial."

Hannah stood still, considering the proposition. He couldn't read her mind, but he knew his idea was a good one. Finally, she consented. "Stay and snoop around, but keep your nose clean. And if I come back to you passed out in bed with a bunch of empty pints of ale lying around on the floor, you'll be swabbing the deck of the *Unlawful* for the rest of your days."

Vitali smiled. "Aye aye, Captain."

Hannah turned toward the door, then looked back at the Lynqi. "And Vitali, don't get hurt. Team BBB needs you."

With that, Hannah from the Boulevard disappeared, leaving Vitali alone.

CHAPTER SIXTEEN

Aysa's leg bounced in anticipation as she stood on the front step of the great hall, waiting for the rest of the crew. Bells continued to peal through the air. Between their chimes, she heard shouts of the citizens blocks away from where she stood. It took everything she had to stay put and follow Hannah's commands.

After what felt like an hour, Parker and Karl stepped out into the sun, each of them gripping their weapons, their eyes sharp and their tempers high. Hannah and Sal landed right behind them.

"No Vitali?" Aysa asked.

Hannah shook her head. "He's going to stay behind and see if he can gather some intel. Things don't seem as squeaky-clean as Kirill wants us to think they are in the royal household. If anyone can sniff out what is truly going down, it's Vitali."

"Like finding a mouse." Aysa giggled. "He'll be sorry when I come back with my stories of conquest. Let's go already."

Hannah gave her a nod, and Aysa gave Parker a playful slap to the back of the head. "Last one there's a lump of rotten remnant shit." She laughed as she took off down the street.

In just a few strides, she opened a healthy distance between Parker and her. Karl had given up before the race began.

Looking over her shoulder, she could see the young Arcadian laughing as his legs pumped like pistons to try to catch the girl from Baseek. He didn't stand a chance, and Aysa knew it. Even though he was a natural athlete, Parker would still be outpaced.

Just for fun, she cut across the street toward a grocery stand. Showing off a little, she leapt off an empty cart and over a tower of fruit boxes, landing in a roll before getting back to her feet with an apple in hand. She turned and launched the apple with dangerous accuracy at her friend. "Come on, old man. Or do you need a break?"

She sprinted two more blocks and then turned toward the noise. As she spun around the corner, the acrid smell of smoke hit her nostrils and scratched the back of her throat. The race was fun and games, but now she was entering the land of serious business.

Thirty feet ahead, a giant building with rows and rows of windows was on fire. Flames licked out of broken windows and off the roof. Thick black smoke hovered over the whole place like a giant mushroom. Aysa slid to a stop, but as she did, there was a flash and in a crack of thunder in front of her.

"I beat you," Hannah said with a grin.

"Bullshit! You cheated."

"You use your gifts," Hannah said. "And I'll use mine. All's fair, girlfriend. At least I didn't use that guy." Hannah pointed at Sal, who flew in circles over the burning building.

"Teleportation and a pet dragon? Keep bragging, Supergirl. You want to remind me how hot your boyfriend's abs are while you're at it?" Aysa asked.

Hannah laughed. "Since you mentioned it, they *are* pretty hot. But enough talk. We need to get in there. The building will collapse any minute, and the city guard is doing shit. They need serious help and direction."

"Wait, you mean to tell me that you've already been up there, assessed the situation, and developed a plan?" Aysa asked.

"You're pretty fast, but you're not *that* fast. I beat you three times over." She patted the girl on the shoulder as Karl and Parker joined them. "I need you guys to go up and try to get Irmand to direct the citizens toward safety. He's focusing on a bucket brigade, but his little pails of water are doing next to nothing against this blaze. It's freaking bedlam in there. The guy's gonna get everybody killed. Do whatever it takes to get the people away, no matter what he tells you."

"What are you going to do?" Parker asked through heavy breathing.

"I've got something better than a bucket of water," she said. As she finished speaking, Sal swooped down, losing no speed in his descent. Hannah grabbed his neck as he approached and flung herself onto his back. Before Aysa could say another word, they were gone.

A scream from the burning building grabbed Aysa's

attention. "Parker, go try to get Irmand to divert his men from his impotent bucket party to help the people affected. Karl, you head around back." She pointed toward a window in the front of the building. "I got this one."

Without waiting for the men to reply, Aysa took off for the burning structure. Three stories up, a woman not much older than Aysa leaned out, holding a toddler in the crook of her arm. "Help me! Please!"

Aysa darted to a spot under the window. "Drop the kid. I've got this."

A look of fear and pain crossed the mother's face, but when the flames licked out of the window above her head, she knew she had no other choice. The kid fell toward Aysa, and she tracked its course. With a step to the left, she grabbed the child in her good arm and dropped him gently on the ground.

Looking up, she shouted, "It's your turn."

The woman's eyes darted about. She took a moment to look back into the burning building, but there was no escape that way. The woman pushed her legs out the window and sat with her butt on the sill. Aysa knew exactly what she was thinking—there was no way the Baseeki girl could catch a full-grown woman. She was right. Without a second to lose, she heard a guttural shout from behind her. "I've got ye, lady. Ye can do this."

Aysa turned and saw Karl racing toward them, rolling a giant cart filled with hay in front of him. The woman jumped and hit her mark perfectly. Aysa pulled the woman out, and she clung to her in an embrace. "Thank you. Thank you. You saved me. You saved both of us."

Aysa pushed her away. "It's nothing. That's what we do."

"It's not enough," the woman said. She turned and pointed toward the building. "There are more in there."

Aysa wiped ash off the woman's cheek. "Like I said, it's what we do."

She gave Karl a nod of thanks and rushed for the front entrance of the building. The doorknob glowed red-hot, so Aysa raised her shield, lowered her shoulder, and ran as hard as she could at the barrier between her and the helpless citizens of Solyr. The wood shattered on contact, and she continued into the hellscape.

The fire burned around her, and she could feel smoke stick to her lungs and dry out her eyes. Pulling her shirt up over her mouth, she ran into the blaze as others stumbled out. Nearly getting lost, Aysa went from room to room, helping people limp their way toward safety. She climbed the stairs and cleared the second floor. It wasn't until she was on the fifth floor that she found a child under a bed weeping and shouting for help. Aysa flipped the mattress over, and the boy stared up to her with wide eyes.

"Are we going to die?" he asked.

Aysa kept her face as calm as possible. "Yes. We're all going to die, but as far as I'm concerned, I'm not letting today be your day. Come with me."

Aysa had the little boy climb onto her back, and he gripped her with force likely to suffocate her faster than the smoke. She ran down the hall, dodging flames on the way. Just as she got to the top of the stairwell, she heard the creaking of wood. With a crash, the stairs fell out from underneath them.

"We need to go up. Hang on tight, kid. I'm getting you out of here," she shouted over the roaring of the fire.

Aysa took the stairwell up, heat and smoke chasing her the whole way. She had one hope, and she knew it would not disappoint. It never had.

Gaining the top of the building, she kicked in the door and stumbled out into the night air. Even with the smoke pouring out from the building beneath them, a cool lick of breeze hit her head, and she felt a bit of relief.

Creaking and cracking surrounded them again. Aysa knew the roof wouldn't hold. The building was coming down, and it would take them with it if she didn't figure this out fast. She ran to the edge.

Help, please! she thought as hard as she could. Aysa had no magical powers at her disposal, but she knew Hannah had more than enough for the both of them.

The roof behind her started to fall away; chunks of rock and wood fell into the fire as if they were trying to fill in a volcano. She glanced up. Hannah and Sal were more than thirty yards away, and they would not make it.

Aysa held the kid tightly. If it was to be her end, she wanted to give him the comfort she hadn't had when she was his age. But a voice rang in her head. *Do it!*

There are few people in the world that Aysa listened to. Very few.

Hannah was one of them.

Without hesitation, she squeezed the child and jumped off the edge of the seven-story building.

Wind whipped around her, tossing her hair in every direction. She held her breath in case she had trusted in vain, but within feet of the ground, her body and the body of her passenger stopped. They floated, just above the ground, and then, like a feather dropped from a ladder, they drifted down.

She put the child down and looked up toward the smoke-filled sky.

"Thanks, girlfriend," she yelled toward the sky before turning back toward the building.

CHAPTER SEVENTEEN

"Don't be an asshole, Irmand," Parker yelled over the noise of death and destruction.

The captain of the guard just stared at him. Parker knew the look. It was the countenance of a man beaten by his circumstances. Parker had no time to debate within himself about whether Irmand was simply a fool or the product of a system that had failed him.

"I've got to put this fire out," he shouted and turned back to his bucket brigade. Twenty soldiers stood in a line, passing along water from a nearby well.

"Your buckets are doing no good. You need to get the people out of there."

But Irmand was done listening.

"Fine. If you won't do it, I will," he said and turned toward the building.

Parker navigated around the edge and toward the back side of the apartment complex. If there was one thing that he knew after his years of working with the Bitch and Bastard Brigade, it was that they were all better when they worked together. Rounding the second corner, he saw Karl hammering at a wall with his trusted weapon. As he approached the rearick, Karl stepped back and looked up into Parker's eyes. He was exhausted. Nearly spent.

"I'm glad yer finally here, lad. The entrance has collapsed, and there's still folk inside. I'm gonna need yer help to get us in there. I hate to say it, but I can't do it on me own."

"We weren't made to do anything on our own, Karl. What do you need?"

Karl raised a finger and pointed at a spot along the outer wall. "Focus yer energy right there. We should be able to carve out an openin' without bringin' the whole damned buildin' down. Give me a blast. That should do it."

Parker leveled his spear at the spot Karl had indicated, and when he pulled the trigger, a clean, solid blast of blue energy hit the brick. The wall shook but didn't fall.

"Again, lad!"

Parker pulled the trigger again. Brick blasted in all directions, but the wall held firm.

"Okay. Stand back," Karl yelled.

The rearick stepped up and swung his hammer with the vigor of a man twenty years younger. Parker could only imagine his friend two decades ago in the mines trying to find the precious stones that made half the modern world run.

Again and again, he struck the spot. His aim was perfect. Finally, the wall crumbled, and smoke poured out of the hole.

Karl panted, and Parker expected his heart to burst right then.

"Aye, let's get 'em out of there."

The two men scrambled over the rubble into the burning building. Parker pulled the trigger on his spear again and the tip of it glowed like a hundred flames. He heard Hannah's voice in his head. *Near the back.* Parker followed her prompting and found a group of people huddled in the corner, all of them holding useless rags over their mouths.

"Come with me," he shouted, leading them out of the building toward the new opening Karl had created.

Once that round of people was evacuated from the burning building, Parker rushed back in to see if there were more. Eyes burning from the smoke, he stumbled toward a room in the rear of the building. Three people came into the orb of light cast by the blue amphoralds at the tip of his spear, two women nearly dragging an older man between them, their shoulders sagging under his weight.

"You're almost there," Parker encouraged them on. "Do you need my help?"

The stately old woman looked at her younger partner and her eyes flashed yellow. As Parker watched, her body expanded, growing before his eyes. She straightened her back, and the man almost left his feet under her height. In response, the other woman did the same.

"That's pretty badass. I think you've got this," Parker said to the Mylek women.

As they escaped the flames, Parker pushed farther in and down the hall.

Parker cut through the thick smoke, his elbow covering his nose and mouth, trying to keep it out of his lungs in vain. Getting to the other side, he searched for his rearick friend.

"*Scheisse*, Parker. I never thought I'd be so glad to see yer ugly mug." Karl coughed from across the room.

"Karl?" Parker's eyes darted around the place. His amphorald torch fought to cut through the thick black smoke.

"Down here, ye bastard."

Almost immediately at his feet, under a giant wooden beam, lay his friend.

"All these years of fightin' bastards in every corner of Irth. I never thought me demise would come at the hand of a twelve-by-twelve hunk of lumber. Can ye get this thing off me, mate?" Karl wheezed.

Parker grabbed the smoldering wood. The heat licked at his hands, but he pushed the pain out of his mind. Squatting, he got into just the right position to try a dead-lift. The wood didn't budge. He tried again, feeling the muscles in his legs, ass, and back strain against the impossible weight.

"Try yer spear," Karl shouted.

Parker stepped back and aimed his weapon at the timber but didn't pull the trigger. "Too risky. You'd likely get caught in the blast."

Karl nodded. "There's not enough time. The ceiling's gonna give and take us both out. Ye gotta get outta here."

Parker shook his head. "Not a chance, old friend." He jammed his spear under the beam and pushed with his shoulder. Still, even with the leverage, it hardly moved.

"Go, Arcadian. Save yerself. If ye die with me in this room, Hannah is gonna chase both of us all the way to the

River Styx and kick our damn asses fer bein' so stupid. Now go!"

Parker gripped Karl's shoulder. "Don't go anywhere; I'll be right back."

He traced his steps back the way he came in, sprinting through the fiery furnace as quickly as his legs would take him. Breaking out the hole he and Karl had made, Parker gasped fresh air. He cast his eyes around the group gathered just beyond the heat of the fire.

"I need your help," he yelled at the two women who had just escorted a man out of the building.

They were standing in front of him before he had the chance to ask a second time. "What do you need?"

"Muscle," Parker answered. "A lot of it."

The woman smiled at each other knowingly. "Muscle, we can do."

A man wearing the colors of the royal family approached them. "I'm in too," he said. "I can't get big and strong like these two, but my physical magic is significant."

"Let's go," Parker said as he led them back into the blaze and toward Karl.

When he finally stood over his friend, he saw that the rearick's face was still, his eyes closed. It was too late. A knot twisted in Parker's stomach.

Karl's eyes snapped open. "Aye, ye shitehead. I told ye to get outta here and stay out. Now ye've brought these good folk into my hell." He looked around the room. "Or have we both passed into Hades?"

Parker directed the Mylek women to shift into their strongest form possible. Their eyes flashed yellow as they bulked up to twice their normal size. One of the women turned her hands over in front of him, and thick calluses like leather gloves formed across her palms.

Wasting no time, he jammed his spear under the wooden beam and flexed with all his might as the women worked their own deadlift. He could feel movement; it was starting to budge—but not enough. It wasn't until the Myrna man turned his magical attention to the wooden beam, eyes glowing black, that the thing started to move. Parker knew he was applying just enough telekinesis to make the difference.

Karl grunted. "I'll be damned." He shifted his body out from under the smoldering beam. "Ye did it."

"We all did it," he corrected.

Parker and the Myrna man helped Karl to his feet, and the women led the way out of the destruction. As they were leaving the room, the ceiling began to crumble and fall, but as the debris plummeted toward their heads, it hit a shimmering blue shield and deflected around them. Parker looked over his shoulder at the man, whose eyes were still glowing, and gave him a nod of thanks.

Once they were back outside, Parker and Karl dropped into the dusty yard. Smoke still hung around their heads, but they had made it as far as they could. Both men were exhausted.

"Are you going to be okay?" Parker asked.

"How's me beard?"

"Your what?"

"Me beard, dammit. Last time I fought a fire, I lost me beard. The Baseeki didn't stop makin' fun a me fer weeks."

Parker laughed. "Your beard's fine. I'm more worried about your chest."

Karl snickered. "Nothin wrong with me chest. Didn't even have much weight on this big ol' barrel of mine. It just had me pinned real good." He pointed to the two Mylek women and the Myrna man. "If it weren't for them folk, I'm sure I wouldn't have made it out of that place alive, and I imagine Parker here would have been barbeque right alongside me."

The older woman gave a slight smile and nodded her head. "With all you're doing for us, there's no way I could have left you in there. If there's anything else I can do, don't hesitate to ask."

"I could use a drink. Sure am thirsty."

"You're always thirsty," Parker said.

"When yer right, yer right. And it wouldn't be so bad if some of the smoke cleared out of me eyes. Can ye call up a major gust?" Karl grinned.

Parker shifted up onto his elbows and looked at the burning building. "Right. We could use some rain, too."

No sooner than he had said the words than the sound of rushing wind came from behind them. Karl tilted his head back and watched the underside of the dragon as he flew over.

"Ye think she can hear everything we say?"

Parker shrugged. "Doesn't matter much. I mean, she can read our damned minds anyway."

"Some girlfriend ye got," Karl said.

Parker smiled, then said extra loud just in case she was listening, "Don't I know it. She's the best."

CHAPTER EIGHTEEN

"All right, lizard, let's finish this," Hannah yelled, gripping Sal's back with her thighs.

The dragon banked left and swooped toward the crowds who had gathered around the building. There were hundreds, maybe thousands watching the building burn. Hannah guessed that most of the town was there, many of them rushing around looking for loved ones. An audible gasp swept the crowd as Sal crossed the mass of humanity.

"And they thought Vitali looked weird," Hannah commented, giving Sal a pat on the side of the neck. His mighty wings flapped in rhythm as they climbed toward the top of the building. The flames still raged, and the smoke billowed into the air. Bright red embers spat beside her. Hannah threw one bolt of ice after another to try to cool the fire, but it was out of control.

Sal gave his right wing an extra beat, banking them to the left. As they edged around the pillar of smoke, Hannah saw the most imminent danger to the city. She thought that the fire would be contained, but the flames were edging to the south, threatening a lower complex of structures.

"Take me up above the fire, Sal. Time to make it rain."

He obeyed, and soon they were soaring above the thickest billows of smoke. Their position allowed Sal to fly tight circles over the inferno. At first, Hannah had expected to just let the fire burn itself out. The building was beyond saving, after all. She thought that maybe if she created a little wind, the city might experience a respite from the suffocating cloud, but the spreading of the flames worried her. Wind might do more damage than good. It was time to manipulate nature, and she would need all her strength for the deluge that was required.

As Sal circled, the magician raised her arms above her head, and her eyes glowed brilliant red. She concentrated on all the people who had lost loved ones that day. She thought of the town in turmoil. She thought of her team fighting for the people of this foreign land, and as she focused on these things, a longing welled up in her guts and moved toward her chest—a deep and abiding love for the people. Not only her people, but for all people in Irth.

As the love grew, Hannah could feel her power strengthening. She focused it toward the sky. Hair stood up on the back of her neck as the first bolt of lightning struck.

"Come on," she yelled at the air. "Give me what I want."

She concentrated more intently and willed a change in the fabric of the universe.

Another lightning strike. A fierce gust of wind. A thunderclap that shook her bones.

And then it began: one drop, then another, and within a

few beats of a dragon's heart, the skies opened and loosed their wet mercy.

Hannah laughed as the rain washed down over her head, cleansing the filth from her skin. She leaned down and hugged Sal.

They circled a half-dozen times to keep an eye on the progress. When it was clear that the heavy rains were going to do their job, Hannah nudged Sal toward the ground. Flying in, she could see a thousand faces. Shock and awe were written on each one.

Sal, never one to waste an audience, made a perfect landing. Digging in his heels, he slid to a stop, then tilted his head back and let out a mighty roar.

Hannah jumped off her dragon's back and stood before the crowd.

They stared in silence, until at last, a single voice shouted, "All hail the Matriarch!"

CHAPTER NINETEEN

"Man, you're a freakin' rock star," Aysa remarked as the crowd continued to chant for Hannah. "They love you. Guess they'll need another big-ass statue in the middle of town."

Parker raised a brow. "Maybe not. They think she *is* the Matriarch, which is a little creepy for her boyfriend."

"Aye, Parker. I guess when ye put it that way, it gives a whole 'nother meanin' to 'mommy issues.' But ye'll need to work on that one with yer woman." Karl scanned the crowd, which was impressive, if not a little frightening in its heightened admiration of Hannah and her crew. Among them, one face stood out, and it was moving directly toward them. "Well, seems one feller in the bunch still has his arsehole puckered."

Irmand stood before the BBB, his hand gripping his club like a vice, face pale, and his lower lip trembling. In response, Karl slung his hammer onto his shoulder at the ready, just in case the man was looking to do something utterly stupid. No one in their right mind would step up to

Hannah and her team after what they had just seen, but Irmand had seemed a few pints short of a keg since the day they met him.

"The hell was all of that?" Irmand shouted in Hannah's direction.

She opened her mouth to respond, but the captain beat her to it and answered his own question. "It was the most impressive use of magic and muscle I've ever seen within our walls. Thank you."

Karl could tell Hannah was practicing restraint. They had all risked their lives while Irmand and his team were passing around leaky buckets.

Hannah extended her hand to the captain of the guard, and he shook it. "It was not only a pleasure, but our responsibility," she replied. After a beat, she continued, "But...you might want to reconsider your approach. Your men could have been better utilized evacuating the building and tending to the people."

Irmand's face grew red. "I understand you see it that way, but a call had to be made. We were trying to keep the fire from spreading beyond the walls of the structure. Better cities than this one have been leveled by the ravaging power of fires." His own words breathed some confidence back into him, and the captain stood tall. "And it is not like I can create a heavenly firehose from the back of a dragon. You *do* realize you had some advantages there."

Clearly, Irmand was not the man Karl had first thought he was. The captain was gruff, certainly, but now it also seemed clear that he had good intentions. Maybe he was even good-natured.

Hannah smiled. "I do not mean to offend, Irmand. And

you are right, I have some," she cleared her throat, "advantages."

"You do." He grinned beneath his bushy mustache. "And of course, one of them is that team of yours. Bravest bastards I've seen in a while!"

"Don't forget us bitches, Tough Guy!" Aysa called.

Finally, Irmand's face broke into a full smile. "Yes, ma'am. Of course. Not sure why, but these days, I can't keep the best of my men. No sooner does a good officer join then he ends up leaving the guard. Hell, almost all of them end up leaving town."

"Deserters?" Parker asked.

Irmand shrugged. "Not sure what to call 'em. They just never show up for work again. Anyway, we might have different approaches, but Solyr would have suffered more greatly had you not been here—or if you chose not to help. I'm grateful. We owe you."

"You owe us nothing, and it looks like there's more work to be done." She nodded toward the scores of people injured in the fire. "If you'll allow, I can spread some of the healing magic of our druids around."

Without waiting for an answer, Hannah left them to serve the people.

Irmand shook his head. "Healing power? Now, that's something. Can she do *everything*?

Karl snorted. "We haven't found her limits yet."

CHAPTER TWENTY

Men and women in loose-fitting clothing ran around the building, some spreading news about the fire in the city, some looking like they were battening the hatches in case the waves of flame a half-mile away decided to devour them all. Vitali moved easily through the chaos.

He pulled his hood tighter around his head. The rooms Kirill had found for them contained a full wardrobe, and it didn't take the Lynqi long to find something that fit him, while also covering most of his fur. It was a blessing that people in this city liked their clothing long and loose, and he had seen plenty of people wearing draped hoods or oversized hats.

The fashion worked to his advantage.

It wasn't the same as stalking prey in the jungle, but there were similar principles involved. Move slowly, stick to the shadows, blend in.

He didn't have a specific destination in mind, although he avoided Myrna children. He imagined that anything out of the ordinary around the great hall would stick out to him if he kept his eyes open and his ears alert.

In the end, it was his nose that led him to his goal.

He smelled death in the air.

Several winding passages away from the throne room was a small, dimly lit chamber. Unlike the rest of the great hall, this room was sparsely furnished. A few ordinary candles illuminated the space's only feature: a body lying as still as death on a table.

Vitali took in the room, then stepped closer.

He had seen plenty of dead bodies of both the furry and furless varieties. This man's body had been altered somehow—painted around the face to give it extra color and dimension, a caricature of life.

This was the king. Even in death, there was no mistaking the royal treatment.

Vitali walked around the body of Aurel. He was not old, not the large graying figure Vitali had expected. He was strong, full of life even, minus the whole death thing.

Vitali wondered what could have killed such a man.

There were no head wounds, as far as he could tell. No bruises around the neck, even under the paint. Vitali reached for the silk cloth covering the body and began to move it back.

"You won't find anything under there."

Vitali spun into a crouch, reaching for the knife at his belt, but the woman before him didn't appear to be a threat, even if Vitali knew better than to trust appearances.

She was old, her body hunched by a lifetime of stooping. Or maybe that was a result of the body magic practiced by the Mylek. She had huge feet, and although they were wrapped in layers of thick cloth, Vitali could see they weren't shaped like most of the furless' feet were.

Her hands too were overlong, like they had been stretched. Her fingers seemed to extend too far to properly hold the broom. Apparently some of the Mylek couldn't hide their changes, like Ky and the other nobles were able to do. Or maybe a lifetime of altering one's body had side effects.

"I didn't see you," Vitali said.

"A habit of mine." She looked Vitali up and down, her eyes slowing as they crossed his furred face and exposed hands. "My name is Nijah. I'm used to keeping a low profile. They prefer it that way."

"It seems we have that in common, Nijah. I am called Vitali." He nodded toward the king's body. "What did you mean by that? What won't I find under there?"

"Evidence." She leaned the broom against a wall and shuffled toward him. "I've worked in this building a long, long time. Since before Aurel took the crown from *his* father. Aurel was a good king, nicer than his predecessor, at least. He often stopped to say hello when he passed me in the halls, and he chatted with me like I was his equal. Told jokes and listened to mine." Nijah laughed, a sharp, sad sound that echoed in the small chamber. "He always seemed to know what the punchline was going to be before I got to it. He was like that with all his people. He knew their needs and worked to provide them, Myrna and Mylek alike."

She placed her hands on his chest. "I was here the night he died. They dragged him in covered in blood. None of the other servants were awake, so I volunteered to wash and prepare the body. It's custom in these parts to send off our dead looking as much like they looked in life as we can."

"Where I come from," Vitali offered, "we let nature take us as we are."

She nodded. "Maybe that's a kindness for those left behind. I wept as I worked. But the damned thing was, there wasn't a wound on him. No cuts, no stabs, no broken bones. Nothing but the blood covering his skin that should have been on his insides."

Vitali stared at the body anew. The Muur of his homeland could kill without leaving a mark, their poisons as sure a death as an arrow to the heart or a slit jugular. He had also spent enough time around magic to know that not every weapon was physical.

He began to ask her about the magic in this city, but something else she said struck him.

"You said he was dragged in. What does that mean? I thought he was killed in the great hall?"

The woman shook her head. "I don't know where he died, but it wasn't here. One of his guards carried him in from the darkness and showed him to Irmand and Kirill. The prince, he ordered me not to tell anyone what I saw. Just to do my work and to keep silent."

Vitali eyed the woman. She was old, but she wasn't weak. There was fire behind her eyes.

"If you were ordered to be quiet, why are you telling me?"

"Because screw that guy," she said angrily. "I saw you with the one who looks like the Matriarch. You're here to help. It's not much, but I want to aid your work any way I can. Aurel was a good king. He shouldn't have died like this."

"Talking to me could be risky."

She laughed again. "They killed the king. A man powerful enough to do that could kill anyone he wanted."

CHAPTER TWENTY-ONE

After healing the worst-hurt people on the grounds outside the apartment building, Hannah paused to look over the effects of the fire on the community. People still shifted throughout the city streets, looking for loved ones and taking account of the damage. She saw Sal aiding in the removal of rubble from the base of the building. Contrary to the jokes, the beast was far from lazy, and he was moved by compassion.

Hannah walked toward a gymnasium across the street, where the other survivors had been moved. Parker joined her.

"How do you feel?" he asked. "I mean, how's your power holding out?"

"I feel fine."

Parker raised his eyebrows. "Yeah. I sometimes forget how much juice you have running through that blood of yours ever since New Romanov. I guess the upgrade was pretty sweet."

"It's useful, especially in times like these. I'll be able to help a lot of people."

"Most of the time, I think you're normal," he told her.

Hannah jabbed him in the shoulder with a tight fist.

He winced. "What was that for?"

"Never call your girlfriend 'normal.'" Hannah winked.

Parker laughed. "Point taken."

A girl in her twenties took Hannah by the arm and walked her toward a group of people on the floor who were reclining on worn workout mats. As Hannah walked past the victims, who had mild burns, her eyes glowed and her fingertips brushed their skin. Immediately, the redness of the burns disappeared, and the blisters shrank.

A boy who was hardly in his teens bowed his head when she passed, saying, "Praise be."

Hannah paused and crouched next to him. She put her fingers under his chin and raised his eyes to hers. "Praise be the Matriarch, but I'm not her. In fact, you probably won't believe this, but not that long ago, I was a lot like you. I was just a kid playing in the slums of *my* city. We all have this power inside us."

The kid laughed. "Not like yours."

Hannah smiled. "Maybe not *exactly* like mine, but you don't have to be like me to make a difference. Work to grow the power you do have into something greater and remember to use it well. Use it for good."

The kid remained silent but nodded. Hannah wasn't sure if she had gotten to him, but she had made it her goal not to become a new god among foreign people. She told her story as briefly as she could and tried to inspire people to greater heights than they thought possible. It was helpful that Ezekiel had spent so much time telling her about how the power worked and how someone could channel it.

She continued down the row, healing people as she went, only stopping when she got to the end. There she found a middle-aged woman slumped against the wall. As Hannah drew closer to her, she could see that the woman's body, her arms, and her legs were misshapen—not quite natural—and her skin was covered with burns.

"She is in bad shape," Hannah's guide said.

As Hannah knelt to grant her healing, another woman about the same age crouched next to her.

"What happened here?"

The woman looked at her ailing friend with admiration. "She's a Mylek like me. When everybody was running out of the building, she ran in. The strength of my people is not only in their bodies. We can shift and change shape, but our real power is in our hearts. Natalia here paid the price for her courage, and I know she would have paid it again and again if she could."

Hannah leaned over the wounded hero. She could feel the power welling up in her body, rejuvenated by a love so deep it would sacrifice its own being for the sake of others. Hannah pushed her healing power out over the woman. Opening her eyes, she saw that the swelling was going down and the bright red splotches were fading, but it would take more.

"Over here already," a voice cried from off to her right. Hannah spun to find Parker by her side. They both stared at a man sitting above the others in a comfortable chair positioned especially for him.

"Just leave her. You've spent enough time on those people," he said with ire in his voice.

Parker gripped her arm, knowing Hannah lacked patience for men like him. Their presumption and disregard for others reminded her of the noble class in Arcadia and the way they had treated Hannah and her friends like animals. "Keep it cool," he whispered. Then he shouted back to the man. "She'll be with you when she can, sir."

He laughed. "She's wasting her magic on those Mylek freaks."

Parker rose to his feet. "I said, wait your damn turn."

"So much for keeping it cool," Hannah whispered back.

"You hear that, Irmand?" the man shouted. "This outsider is threatening me!"

"Well," Irmand said. "You're the one acting like a jackass."

The man's face turned red. "Kirill will hear about this. First you let these Mylek start the fire, then you let them suck up even more of our resources."

"That's a lie," the woman on Hannah's left said.

"It's true," a Myrna woman shouted. "I saw it myself."

Hannah felt Parker tense. There was going to be another brawl.

"Everyone shut the hell up," Irmand shouted, "or you'll be dealing with me." His eyes turned black, and he gripped his club in his hand. Hannah could see the unease on everyone's face, but the fight stopped there.

The captain of the guard turned toward the Myrna man. "You'd better get out of here. Make sure you throw a bandage on those burns before sending in your report."

The man rose and walked away, grumbling.

Irmand looked at the Myrna woman. "What do you know?"

"I saw it all start," she said. "It was a group, a big group of Mylek wearing those blue scarves over their faces. I didn't think much of it. I mean, I've heard of the Blue Scarves. Petty vandals, that's all I thought they were. Five minutes later, the smoke started to pour out of the windows. Five more after that, it was bedlam."

Hannah listened and asked Irmand, "What's this all about?"

Irmand sighed. "We've been getting reports like this for weeks. A group of Mylek wearing blue scarves to cover their faces is causing trouble all over town. My men, the ones I have left, have been chasing down leads for days, with no results to speak of. If anyone knows anything, they're not talking. The Blue Scarves' activity has really ramped up since King Aurel died. Messages have been dropped at my office and also at Kirill's. They say they won't stop until the king's killer is brought to justice, which means this fire might only be a taste of what's to come."

"You really can't find any leads?" Parker asked. "Someone in the Mylek community has to know something."

Irmand laughed. "That man was right. You *are* a foreigner. The Mylek don't particularly like my men and me. My guess is that they're covering for the Blue Scarves."

"That's bullshit," the woman Hannah was healing said. She struggled to sit up. "Those radicals don't speak for us."

"Yeah, Captain," another Mylek man said. "If you didn't

notice, that apartment building was full of mostly Mylek. We're not wild enough to burn our own."

"Of course," Irmand said, his face turning pink. "I didn't mean to suggest..."

"It's just like the Myrna," the woman repeated. "Blame us Mylek for everything that goes wrong in the city."

"It's okay," Hannah said, putting her hand on the woman's forehead. "I'm here to fix some of those wrongs."

The woman smiled and closed her eyes as Hannah's healing power rushed over her. She turned back to Irmand. "Why don't you share what intel you do have with us? We'd be more than happy to help you."

"Just add it to the list," Parker added.

Irmand rubbed his beard. "Why would you do that? What's in it for you?"

Hannah smiled. "We're the Bitch and Bastard Brigade. It's what we do."

CHAPTER TWENTY-TWO

The sun had finally gone down by the time the BBB convened again in front of the burned-out building. Parker dropped down on his ass, exhausted from patching people up and helping others look for their loved ones. He couldn't get Irmand's words out of his mind.

This fire is the tip of what's to come.

Karl and Aysa sat on either side of him. Hannah remained standing.

Poor Sal had dropped, exhausted, on the grass, his scaled body now serving as a playground for a group of Mylek street kids.

Aysa's eyes were locked on the building, which still showed red embers that would continue to glow for days. "Anybody have any marshmallows?" She laughed.

"*Scheisse!* Too soon, Freak Girl."

She dropped onto her back and stared up at the sky. "We need a little humor, rearick. It's how you make it through."

Parker listened to them banter back and forth, but his

mind was still on the exchange between the Myrna and the Mylek. It seemed that the Myrna had all the power in this town, which was just another thing to remind him of Arcadia during his lifetime. Naturally, he assumed the Mylek were on his side. His people. But he tried to remember that things were not always as they seemed.

"Yeah," Hannah said. "It does feel a lot like Arcadia."

Parker laughed. "Can you at least tell me when you're in my mind?"

"Sorry, hot stuff. I just can't keep my mind off you."

"It's not quite as bad as yer old days in Arcadia. At least there ain't those sonsofbitch Hunters goin' 'round brandin' people."

"Yeah," Aysa added, "and nobody's gotten her hand cut off, either."

Karl snorted. "That wasn't in Arcadia."

"Okay, sure. Now my disability doesn't matter? Great."

Parker ignored their exchange. "As far as we know, Aurel was a good ruler. Maybe the next king will bring them a little closer to Arcadia."

"I don't know if this town will survive long enough to become rotten through and through," Aysa said. "As far as I can tell, these people are ready to tear each other limb from limb. There's more tension here than on the *Unlawful* when Sal sneaks into the stash of kaffe."

"So, what do we know?" Hannah asked.

"Clearly," Parker said, "the Myrna hold the power in this town."

"And they're clearly dicks," Aysa added.

Karl shook his head. "Not all of 'em. One of them Myrna helped get that damn beam off me chest. Not sure if

Parker and his lady friends could have done it without a lil' physical magic from that one."

"Lady friends?" Hannah asked.

Parker pushed a hand through his ash-crusted hair. "When you've got it, you've got it. What can I say? Try not to get too jealous, babe."

"Oh, I'll try." She laughed. "So, the Myrna… They know at least rudimentary physical magic. And the Mylek?"

"Aye, lass. Them's the most impressive ones. They've got a magic I've heard of but ne'er seen. They change their bodies into all sorts of things, with massive hulkin' muscles, claws, thick hides."

"I swear I saw one with spikes coming out of her back," Aysa said. "Freaking awesome."

"And damn strong, too," Karl added. "I'm surprised they're not the ones runnin' the show round here."

Parker looked at Hannah. "I don't know. I wouldn't underestimate the power of physical magic."

Hannah nodded. "So, how do we settle all this without testing which type of magic, body or physical, is the stronger? We need to help these people make peace before they burn this city to the ground."

"We can't do that until we find out who killed the king," Parker countered. "And who's behind these Blue Scarf attacks."

Karl shrugged and patted the weapon hanging at his side. "'At's all well and good, but ye know I'm much better when I have a clear baddie to swing me hammer at."

Hannah nodded. "Me too, Karl. Me too. Let's hope Vitali has gotten a line on that little mystery."

CHAPTER TWENTY-THREE

Prince Kirill wasn't a hard man to find.

After speaking with the old Mylek woman, Vitali decided he would spend some time getting to know their generous host. The prince stormed around the great hall like he owned the place, which, Vitali figured, wasn't far from the truth. And everywhere he went, he made his presence well known.

As far as Vitali could tell, Kirill's job was to talk, and Kirill seemed to work a lot. Even when his meetings were private, Kirill's booming voice made it easy to pick up on the central details. The funeral was the main thing on Kirill's mind. Day one of the three-day waiting period was almost over, which meant Team BBB didn't have much time. Aurel would be laid to rest, and an election would determine Solyr's fate.

Either the city would find its way forward, or the Myrna and the Mylek would tear each other to pieces.

While Vitali couldn't say he liked Kirill, at least not with a straight face, it was hard to see anything sinister in the man's actions. The funeral needed to take place, and the city needed to elect a new ruler. Kirill played the part of a politician through and through, big smiles and all.

Vitali felt the urge to punch that big smile right down the prince's throat.

As night descended upon the great hall, the Lynqi didn't even consider abandoning his watch. Night meant fewer people and less light, which meant he was freer to operate. He hoped he could get closer to his quarry, and maybe catch him in an unguarded moment.

The night was made for spilling secrets, and Kirill did not disappoint.

After speaking to a group of merchants about increasing food stores for the funeral, Kirill said good night to all other inquisitors and closed up the great hall. He then retired to his private study, a secure room a stone's throw from the throne.

It took Vitali several minutes to find a way in, but there was a small crawlspace between the decoratively arched ceiling and the second floor with enough cracks in it that Vitali could partially see the prince and hear anything spoken above a whisper. Vitali moved slowly across the hard wood until he was in place.

And then he waited.

It didn't take long for him to be rewarded.

A knock rang against the door to Kirill's office, and without getting out of his chair, he called for the person to enter. Irmand, the captain of the guard, stepped in. The large man stepped in front of Kirill's desk and stood at attention.

"Well?" Kirill asked with an air of boredom. "Any news to report?"

"Yes, sir." Irmand cleared his throat. "The fire in the east district was almost certainly caused by foul play. At least one witness claims to have seen the Blue Scarves, but I have been unable to verify that."

"Oh, it was most certainly those little bastards. They would love nothing more than to see this city burn. I know they're being protected since those Mylek scum watch out for their own."

"I will take care of it, sir."

"You damn well better," Kirill said. He slammed his hand on the table. "This should have been dealt with weeks ago. If you can't handle this mess, I'll find someone who can. Are we clear?"

"Yes, sir."

"Good." Kirill leaned back in his chair. "Now, tell me about the girl. Will she be a problem?"

"I…" Irmand paused for a second. "It is unclear. She is as powerful as we were led to believe, there is no denying that. She saved lives today."

"But why?" Kirill asked, shaking his head. "Why is she here? Why would she so graciously deign to help us? This is why you would make a piss-poor politician, Irmand. You have no imagination, no instinct for asking the right questions. I don't trust this Hannah or her Bastard Brigade. No one as strong as that acts solely for the sake of others. No one. If she can help around the city, fine. I'll allow it. But she is an outsider, and I won't have her interfering with our work. Understood?"

"Yes, sir."

"And your men. You'll be able to keep them in line? I've heard reports about desertion and dissention in the ranks."

Irmand stood a little taller as he spoke. "They'll stay in line, or they'll get to know the business end of my club, sir."

"What about that man, the one who was there when—"

"Thaed has been let go from the force, obviously, but I paid him well for his discretion. He'll keep quiet, and no one will believe him anyway if he talks."

"He had better not. No one can know what Aurel was doing that night. No one. Not until after the election, at least. After that, the truth won't matter. And then this Queen Bitch wannabe can fly off to wherever the hell she came from."

Thaed, Vitali repeated the man's name to himself. *It sounds like I might need to pay this man a visit.*

CHAPTER TWENTY-FOUR

"I don't know, Karl. It wouldn't be such a bad city to settle down in," Aysa said as they wove through side streets toward the edge of town. "I mean, if you got rid of the king's murder, bigotry, and terrorists, it would probably be pretty freakin' cool."

"Of course, ye'd think that. I mean, ye've never really known a home, have ye?"

Aysa thought about that for a minute. The village she grew up in had never cared for her. And now, while following Hannah all over the world, putting down roots just wasn't much of an option.

"The *Unlawful*'s my home," she finally decided.

"It's a damn ship. An oversized coffin. Can't be yer home," Karl grumbled.

"Anyway, what's wrong with this city?"

"Well, like ye said, regicide and terrorists, and that's just the beginnin'."

"Okay, so what else?"

"It's damn hot down here in the lowlands. Hell, we're pretty far south of anyplace where me body feels comfortable. Air as thick as stew. Bugs. No mountains. Warm ale."

"Warm ale?" Aysa asked.

"Well, it ain't as cold as it is up in the Heights, that's fer sure." Karl grinned. "I know what ye think. I'll never find a place like the Heights."

Aysa smiled. "Am I right?"

"Probably are."

"Why didn't you head back home with Hadley? You could be there now, unless he ran into some real shit along the way."

"Knowing Hadley, he likely did." Karl paused and checked the directions an attendant had written down for them. His eyes scanned the streets until he found the side street they needed. He continued walking at a brisk pace. "Hadley tried to get me to go. Maybe he just wanted company on the trip. But if I were up in the Heights, I'd just be sittin' around eatin', drinkin', smokin' me pipe—"

Aysa laughed. "Yeah, sounds like a shit life."

"Aye, a rearick can't live on hedonism alone, but the gods know most of 'em are tryin'. Out here, travelin' with ye, I keep me edge. Not to mention, mission brings meanin' to life. Need a reason for bein'."

"You writing a self-help book, rearick?"

"Maybe I ought to, ye lil' fucker. Ye could learn a thing or two. But it's true, ye know. Maybe me home has become the road, and my way a pilgrimage for makin' Irth a better place."

"Now you sound like a sappy old bastard," Aysa shot

back at him with a wink. She nodded up ahead. "I think that's our place."

They approached a storefront with an old, faded sign swinging in the wind. Hannah had asked them to find the supplies they needed to repair the *Unlawful*. And after pulling people from burning buildings, a nice easy task was exactly what Aysa needed to end the evening.

They reached the door, and it was locked. Aysa looked down at the hours scrawled on the sign. "Oh, come on. Says they don't close for another two hours."

Karl cupped his hands around his eyes as he leaned against the window. He could see someone shifting around in the back room beyond the showroom floor. "Aye, there's someone there." He started to bang on the glass. The man looked up, then the lights in the back room went out, shrouding the place in darkness.

"Son of a bitch," Aysa said. "If we don't get this part for the *Unlawful*, you might just get to see what it's like to settle down in this foreign land after all, Karl."

The possibility must've terrified the rearick since he continued to bang incessantly on the thin glass. The shop owner must have realized that Karl and Aysa were not going away, so he finally came to the front, unlocked the door, and pulled it open.

"I'm sorry, I was just getting ready to close up shop for the day."

Aysa looked him up and down. It wasn't hot, but the man's forehead was covered with sweat. "Closing up early, huh? You got a hot date or something?"

He let loose an uncomfortable laugh. "Happily married

for thirty-five years, so it's a date every night." The man stuffed his hands into his pockets and looked at his feet for a second before saying, "Slow day, that's all. What can I do for you?"

"Well, we have a vessel that runs on the power of amphoralds."

"Amphoralds?" The man's eyes widened. "It's been a long time since I've heard anyone talk about those. I hate to say it, but I don't have anything for that kind of tech. Haven't for years."

"We didn't tell you what we were looking for," Karl said. He elbowed Aysa. "Keep going, kid."

Aysa described the parts that were damaged during the pirate attack and then handed him a sheet of parchment.

The shop owner took the schematic drawn years ago by Gregory's father and moved from the doorway into the light of his shop. He turned the blueprints back and forth. His eyes had a look of recognition, and she saw a little trace of joy brush past his eyes. He cleared his throat and said, "Yes. Unfamiliar, but I can get this for you. It will take some time."

"How much time?" Aysa asked.

The man glanced over his shoulder and then back at Aysa and Karl. "Much time, I am afraid, dear. Weeks. Maybe months. With the pirate activity, our supply chain has been hellishly unpredictable."

He glanced over his shoulder again, and Aysa stood on her tiptoes, trying to see what the man was looking at.

Karl stepped toward the counter and placed both hands on the flat surface. Leaning in, he said, "Yer name's Otto, ain't it?"

The man silently nodded and then tilted his head toward the storeroom again.

"All right, then. Unless there's two Ottos in this town, this here's yer shop, and I imagine ye know it inside and out, if yer worth yer mustard."

"Yes. Yes, sir. And you're welcome in my shop, but you have to understand there are some things I just can't do," the man said, his eyes darting around. Aysa thought she caught a shadow moving in the back room.

Aysa reached behind her and pulled her shield off her back. She held it like a throwing disc by her side. "Otto, I know you want to help us, but it sounds to me like there's something keeping you from offering your assistance. Is that right?"

The man closed his eyes and then snapped them open in some kind of rudimentary code. He and Aysa were on exactly the same page. "No, ma'am. It's just my stock is limited."

Aysa snickered. "Sounds like a personal problem, Otto. Thirty-five years of marriage and all." She lifted her shield and held it parallel with the floor. "Might I suggest you check again? Maybe on the lower shelves?"

Otto hit the floor. Aysa flicked a switch on her shield and launched it through the back doorway and into the dark room.

A bright light flared from its amphoralds in the back storeroom, followed by cursing.

"Now!" she shouted. Before Karl had the chance to scurry around the countertop, Aysa had already vaulted it with her good arm.

Otto was kind enough to hit the lights as they dashed for the back.

As they entered a storeroom lined with shelves and filled with mechanical parts, a figure dressed in black was pulling himself off the ground. He pressed the heel of his palms against a black mask where his eyes would be.

"You broke my nose," he complained.

"Yeah, well, I'll break a lot more if you don't tell me what the hell you're doing creeping around in the dark."

"You don't belong here," he said, his voice distorted by the broken nose.

"Ah, so that's what it's gonna be like," Karl said as he ran into the room. "Then maybe I can shove me hammer where it don't belong. Right up yer arse."

The man held his arms to the side. Aysa could see what looked like two metal gauntlets on them.

"Time to show you how hospitable this city can be."

He charged forward, moving remarkably fast, but instead of swinging as Aysa expected, he pushed his hands forward. A thick layer of ice formed on the ground as Karl raised his hammer. The momentum and the slippery surface sent the rearick sprawling.

Aysa held on just enough to dodge a metal fist to the face. She swung out with her bolas, but the masked man blocked them with his gauntlets. The clang of metal on metal rang through the workshop.

The man moved like he had some serious training. Between his speed, his fists, and his spellwork, he kept Aysa on her toes. It didn't help that she was fighting without her shield, and the bolas were not great defensively.

She dodged a fireball and a fist and stepped backward. The man was pushing her into a corner.

"Here!"

She jumped at Karl's voice and grabbed her shield out of the air. The man swung at her, but her shield took the hit, and then she shoved it forward, pushing the man back.

Right into Karl's hammer.

If Karl had been aiming for a kill, there would have been no way for their attacker to block it. But information was better than blood, and the rearick went easy, which gave the man just enough time to bring up his hands.

Still, the force of Karl's swing sent him sailing into a large wooden crate, and splinters flew in every direction.

Aysa ran toward the hole, but the man was nowhere to be found. She looked around frantically before spotting an open window at the back of the shop.

"That bastard was damn good," Karl said. "Fer a magic user. Not many could stand that long against me, me hammer, and yer balls."

"Yeah, he was good. And if you don't mind, I prefer you call them my 'bolos.'"

"Sure, Aysa." Karl snorted and patted his hammer. "As long as I can still call this girl me sweetheart."

"You men and your fascinations with all things phallic. Call it whatever you want, Shorty. I don't even mind if you sleep with her." She motioned toward the window. "Should we give chase?"

Karl waved his hand in the direction the man had escaped. "Aye, seein' that one fight, I can only imagine he's halfway 'cross the city by now. Let 'em go, and let 'em tell his Myrna friends that if they mess with us, they're gonna get the anger of the Matriarch and her Justice shoved into very uncomfortable places."

"No meaning without mission, ain't that right, Guru?"

Otto joined them from the front of his store. "I-I don't know how to thank you."

Aysa fastened her shield to her back and brushed the dust off her cloak. "I don't know. Seemed like if it wasn't for us, you would've just had a normal business day with a visit from Mr. Douche-in-Black. Somebody has it out for us, that's for sure."

"What do ye know about it?" Karl asked.

Otto leaned against the workbench and smoothed his jacket with both hands. Looking up, he said, "Nothing. I was back here doing inventory when he appeared behind me out of nowhere. As you might've guessed, I'm no fighter. He told me that when the outsiders came for equipment, I needed to send them away empty-handed, or I'd leave here without my hands."

"I guess his timing was a wee bit off," Aysa said. "Now, about that part. How long will it take if we order today?"

Otto laughed. "About fifteen seconds." He walked over to a shelf at the end of the far row. Returning with a faded wooden box, he bowed his head to his friends. "I haven't sold one of these for years. Hell, I thought I'd scrap this one someday soon, but it's yours."

Karl pulled out a leather pouch from his belt and started shaking coins into his hand. "How much do we owe ye?"

"It looks more like I owe you. This one's on the house."

Karl counted out ten coins and stacked them on the

workbench. "The Bitch and Bastard Brigade believes the worker is worth his due, Otto. Yer a good man. Let's hope them arseholes don't come back now that we have what we came looking fer."

"Thank you. And yes, let's hope."

CHAPTER TWENTY-FIVE

Hannah kicked her feet up on the stool and blew across the top of her morning mug of kaffe. The late morning sun warmed her face as she sat on the porch of their wing of the great hall. Surrounded by her friends, she was happy just to have a couple of minutes of peace and quiet after one hell of an introduction to Solyr. It was, after all, the main reason they had stopped in the city. That, and for the part for the *Unlawful* that they were able to procure with some effort. As usual, there was plenty for the Bitch and Bastard's Brigade to do.

"This devil's brew is actually growin' on me." Karl grunted, keeping an eye on Sal. "As long as we can keep it out of that lil' demon, we'll be in great shape."

Sal raised his head and opened his eyes, staring at the rearick. His tongue whipped in and out of his lizard mouth. Hannah laughed when she saw all the muscles in his body tense. "Not a chance, Sal. The Blue Scarves are committing enough terror in the hearts and minds of the citizens. We can't add a hopped-up lizard buzzing around like some overgrown dragonfly to their woes."

Sal dropped his head back between his front legs and closed his eyes. His tail thumped the ground.

While the others sat in their chairs, Aysa stood, leaning against the post and sipping her own cup of kaffe. As if reading Hannah's mind, she said, "What are we going to do today? I can't take all this sitting around."

"All this sitting around?" Parker asked. "I've barely had time to use the restroom since we've landed. I can't imagine you on an actual vacation."

"I thought this was a vacation," Aysa replied. "I'm having a blast. Putting out fires. Fighting magical masked assassins. Maybe we should go explore the hills outside of town. I hear there might be some pirate ass to kick out there."

Hannah pointed toward the city gates. "Looks like we have something to entertain us, at least."

The sound of trotting hooves came to their ears, and soon a horde of creatures ambled down the city streets in their field of vision.

Karl stood, shading his eyes with the flat of his hand as he stared at the creatures. "Aye, what the holy hell are them things?"

Aysa spun, facing the rearick. "What do you mean, Karl?"

"Them beasts. What are they?"

Aysa laughed, pushing her hand against her mouth. "Karl, do you mean to tell me you've never seen a steer before?"

Karl's face went blank. "Heard of 'em. Never seen 'em. That's like one of them cows, then. Right?"

Aysa shook her head. "Steers. Not cows. Steers."

"What the hell is the difference?" Parker interjected.

"A cow is a steer that had a baby," Aysa explained.

Parker tilted his head to the side. "I thought a cow that didn't have a baby was a heifer?" he asked, scratching the side of his face. "A steer is a dude cow you use to make the lady cows pregnant. Right, Hannah?"

Hannah threw a smile at her boyfriend. The morning was getting better and better. "How the hell should I know? I'm a city girl."

"You got it all wrong," Aysa protested.

"Okay, then. What the hell is an ox?" Parker asked.

"An ox is a steer that still has his junk."

"His junk?" Karl asked. "Ye mean his..." Karl held his palms up as if he were holding two gigantic cannonballs. "His bolas?"

Aysa laughed. "Yeah. Exactly. And as far as I know, I don't think you want to eat an ox. You want to eat the steer. Which isn't a cow, or a heifer. Although I think a heifer is pretty good to eat too."

"*Scheisse*! Aysa, how do ye know all this?"

Aysa shrugged. "I like to ask questions. And I have no freaking clue if I have any of that straight. I might be remembering it all ass-backward. But what I do know is that this line of beasts is for the giant feast tonight. One of our attendants told me that. They'll be slaughtered in honor of King Aurel, and the meat will be used for the celebration of his life."

The cattle got closer, and Karl swore under his breath. "But...but...those things are bigger than Sal." The dragon groaned and grumbled without picking up his head. "I thought they'd be more like...you know, like sheep or lambs or something."

"Ah! You know the difference between a sheep and a lamb?" Aysa asked with her eyebrows raised.

Hannah held her hand up. "Bloody enough, already. You two are ridiculous. Let me enjoy my kaffe without another lesson on animal husbandry, for the Matriarch's sake."

"Oh, yeah, sure. I'll stop talking, Hannah. I'll just stand here and act like I'm having fun." Aysa's leg bounced as she watched the cattle.

"Thank you, Aysa," Hannah replied serenely, sipping her brew.

Karl's face twisted in confusion. "Then what the fuck is a neutered pig?"

They all started laughing, Hannah included. She couldn't ask for anything better than this group of people to spend her time with. To travel with. To fight with. But her thoughts and feelings of contentment didn't last. A giant explosion ripped through the morning air from a couple of hundred feet away.

"Oh, come on!" Hannah exclaimed, setting down her cup and getting to her feet.

Parker scanned the city from where they were sitting, and his eyes locked on a rising plume of smoke. "Looks like the Blue Scarves are at it again."

Karl grunted. "Aye, but at what, then? I don't see no kind of destruction."

Aysa pointed at the cattle. They were butting their heads in every direction and kicking up dust. "I think the BS crew is planning a different kind of destruction. Something a little less, well, direct."

"Oh, shit. You're right," Hannah said. Her eyes blazed red. "I don't imagine this will work."

Of all the magical skills Hannah had acquired over her journey, influencing animals was on the low end, even if she had spent time with several druids. It didn't help that these beasts were terrified. She could feel their minds. Sentient. Fearful. Confused. She tried to soothe them, tried to calm the whole lot down. Her magic had no effect.

She was just a city girl, after all.

"Well, I just learned I can't influence cows," Hannah told them.

Aysa sighed. "Sorry, captain, but I really think those are steers. I mean, if they were cows, I'm pretty sure—"

A second explosion interrupted the girl from Bazeek.

The cattle, disturbed by the first explosion, were driven mad by the second. Snorts and sounds of distress filled the air. They kicked and screamed as if they knew slaughter was near.

The men driving the cattle cracked their whips and yelled and shouted and moved the group, but it did no good. These beasts were scared and pissed and ready for action.

"I don't care what they are. We gotta get down there," Parker shouted. "They'll tear this city apart."

A third explosion, closer and louder, rang out, and with that, the stampede began.

"Go!" Hannah commanded.

"What are you going to do?" Aysa asked.

"Find some Blue Scarves."

Aysa was the first off the porch, with Karl not far behind her. Her heart beat rapidly, like it always did when duty called.

"Yeehaw," she shouted, looking over her shoulder. "Let's go, short stuff. We've got some wrangling to do."

"I have no idea what yer talkin' about," Karl shouted through clenched teeth. "And I have no bloody clue what we're gonna do when we catch them things."

"That's half the fun," Aysa shouted. She shot down an alley and scrambled toward the main boulevard. When she got out into the open, she found the stampede running right at her. Eyes wide, she stood her ground, just waiting for contact.

She glanced at Karl, who had just caught up. "Head for the bazaar. I'll try to take them from here, but if they make it through, you'll need to come up with something."

"Yer bloody nuts, Aysa," Karl shouted.

"Maybe, but I'm loving every minute of it!"

The rearick nodded and turned to go. Before he could,

Aysa grabbed his sleeve. "Shit. Wait. Look." She pulled him up a short set of stairs and pointed down the road toward the stampede. Three blocks down, half the herd was taking a side street off the main boulevard.

"Bloody hell!" Karl yelled.

"You're gonna have to go after them."

"Too far, Aysa. Can't make it from here," he wheezed.

"With a little help, you can," Aysa said. "On the count of three, jump."

"I dunno—"

"Three! Jump."

CHAPTER TWENTY-SEVEN

K arl jumped as high as his gravity-challenged body would take him. Aysa, with her long, strong arm, gave him a couple of extra feet. It wasn't until he met his apex that he realized he had no idea what the plan was. Before he started to fall back toward death-by-hooves, talons grabbed him by the shoulders.

"Aye, thanks fer the lift, ye damned newt. Now get me over there!"

Sal complied and banked toward the side street filled with the cows or bulls or steer or oxen or whatever they were.

Sal dropped Karl off with plenty of room to make a plan and execute. The herd was still far away, six or seven blocks, but they sounded closer. Much closer. And Karl could feel the pounding of hooves under his feet.

"*Scheisse!*" Karl yelled as he looked to his left.

A separate wall of beef rushed toward him, and these animals would make contact within seconds. Somehow, the herd had split again. Karl didn't have time to consider what the hell was going on. He pulled his hammer from his belt, turned, and sprinted as fast as his tiny legs would take him away from the oncoming stampede.

It was more than a few seconds before the first one caught him. Karl glanced over his right shoulder, and saw a head lowered, horns dropped to make shish-ka-rearick.

"Didn't think one without a set of balls would have spikes like that," Karl growled.

As the beast prepared to gore him, Karl spun mid-stride and swooped his hammer at the creature, just hard enough to knock it off pace. The plan worked—and the beast hurtled off into a side alley.

This ain't so hard, Karl thought. Only fifty-four more of 'em to go.

He continued to run and knocked a few more of the beasts out on his way. Soon, he realized he wouldn't last long. Either he would drop from exhaustion under the weight of a hundred hooves, or he'd be pierced by the horns. Neither option was ideal.

The herd surrounded him. Karl had sheathed his hammer and was doing everything he could to keep up with them. His legs burned, and his lungs screamed at him. He was gonna lose it, he knew it.

"Karl, up here," a familiar voice yelled.

Karl looked up to find Parker, hanging by his legs from a fire escape ladder, arms dangling just above the head of the steers. Between his hands was his spear, perpendicular to the ground like a giant trapeze.

Karl took three more strides and then jumped, planting his hand on a massive steer next to him to help vault him toward his friend.

"Fewer pints and meat pies might be a good thing." Parker groaned as he pulled Karl up to a small landing on the fire escape.

Karl collapsed and pushed the back of his hand across his brow, wiping away the sweat. His face was beet-red, pulse rate through the roof. "Aye! Though I think a few pints is exactly what I need right now. Just glad ye were there to pull me arse out of trouble, or I'd have ale pourin' out of a hundred holes in me gut."

"I'll buy the brew right after we stop this parade of pissed-off steaks from tearing up the city." He pointed in the direction the steers were running. "If those sons of bitches get to the bazaar, there's going to be some major carnage. Even with the havoc of the Blue Scarves, the bazaar looked to be brimming with people."

Karl looked down as the steers continued to rush past. "Aye, I'm with ye, Arcadian, but I'll be damned if I'm jumping back into that mess. I don't have yer composition after all."

Parker laughed. "I don't think you'll need to, my friend." He whistled between his fingers, and almost immediately, Karl heard the beating wings approaching.

"Well, it's nice yer girlfriend loaned you her ride!"

CHAPTER TWENTY-EIGHT

"Come on, come on," Aysa muttered as she watched and waited for the coming stampede. She had to time things perfectly.

Her heart raced as she counted the seconds.

The lead steer, which had horns nearly as long as Aysa's arm, dropped its head in preparation for attack. A step away, it roared and shot its head toward the sky with every ounce of instinct, prepared to end whatever life stood before it.

But Aysa had other plans. With perfect timing, she leapt. As she did, the steer ran under her, providing its back as a perfect target.

Aysa nailed the landing.

Almost.

"Shit!" she yelled as she bounced off the beast's back and headed toward the ground. At the last moment, she wrapped her long arm over its neck and pulled herself up.

"It's you and me now, tenderloin."

The steer snapped his neck in every direction,

desperate to throw Aysa from his back. With her powerful hand gripping a fold of skin and her legs gripping his ribcage, she wasn't going anywhere.

"All right, buddy, let's work together on this one," she yelled into the steer's ear as they approached an intersection on the thoroughfare right before the bazaar. For the first time, she wished she could trade her martial combat skills for the magic of her druid friend Laurel, but wishing would get her nowhere.

Within a block of the intersection, she kicked her heels into the beast's sides. It responded by picking up the pace. Now a body length beyond the others, Aysa could sense the entire herd surge to keep up with their leader.

"Attaboy!" she shouted. "Or girl. I really have no idea."

A few yards from the intersection, she pulled at his skin with her good arm and leaned with all her weight toward the side street. Her weight and power turned the steer's head, and his body turned with it. Glancing back, she watched the rest of the herd follow their leader away from the bazaar and out toward the southern gate.

"Holy hell! It worked."

Sal swooped low, allowing Parker and Karl to drop to the ground just at the edge of the bazaar. They stood, each with their weapons out and at the ready.

"The hell we gonna do, Park? The gods know we can't fight these fuckers."

He shook his head. "We can' fight them, but maybe we can use the Blue Scarves' strategy. Give me some fodder to blast!"

Karl got the picture and ran over to a mountain of beer barrels stacked outside a bar.

"Forgive me," he called into the heavens as he heaved the barrels into the path of the herd of angry steers.

"Now!" he shouted.

Parker sent a thick, powerful blast of Etheric energy from his spear.

The barrels burst in an array of shrapnel, blue glow, and warm beer. Karl screamed and raised his hammer, but the animals hardly took notice.

"Ah, hell." Parker grunted as he watched them approach.

He was the only thing that stood between the stampede and the morning crowds at the market.

"Get outta there, kid!" Karl yelled.

But Parker held his ground. In a last attempt, he fired at the oncoming horde, dropping a few of them at the front of the line.

Just before he turned to run, his favorite overgrown newt swept in and landed between him and the steers.

With outstretched wings, Sal stood up on his hind legs and gave a roar like none Parker had ever heard. It was enough to send a chill down his spine, even though he'd known the dragon since he was just a little lizard sprouting wings.

He roared again, this time raising his razor-sharp talons.

The steers in the front of the group jammed their hooves into the ground and slid to a stop, and the ones just behind them ran into the wall of beef. For a moment, they stood like an old bug in the Heights found frozen in the ice. A moment later, the lead steer crouched on all fours and bowed its head to the dragon. The rest followed suit.

"Time for that brew." Karl laughed.

"And a little spiked kaffe for King Sal," Parker added.

CHAPTER THIRTY

Finding where the stampede had started was easy. The hay cart that had exploded was still smoldering and was surrounded by earth torn up by the steers. With a flick of her hand, Hannah put out the fire before it could spread.

The perpetrators were close; Hannah could sense them.

She caught movement to her left, but before she could chase it down, she was hit on the back of the head.

It stung, despite her superhuman strength.

Hannah spun to face a large man with a thick shell-like substance covering his oversized arms. A blue scarf covered the lower half of his face.

He swung again, his punches strong enough to break stone and faster than a man that size had any right to be. But Hannah was faster. She caught his fist in the air and twisted his arm to the side. He cried out in pain.

"It was a mistake to come at me alone," Hannah told him.

The man laughed under his scarf. "I'm not alone."

A second later, Hannah was surrounded. Despite the blue scarves covering their faces, Hannah could tell that all ten of them were Mylek from their bright yellow eyes. Some were strong, and others were small and moved fast enough to blur before her eyes. One woman had sharp bones sticking out of her forearms, and there was a man with oddly bent legs who leapt over Hannah and kicked at her like a mule. But regardless of how their body magic manifested itself, they all fought with a blend of passion and precision.

They had been practicing.

Hannah recovered from the surprise attack quickly and showed the Blue Scarves just how fast and strong *she* could be. She held back since there was much she didn't know, and she couldn't risk killing these Blue Scarves until she had her answers. Plus, there was the fear of collateral damage. A group of Solyrians began to peek their heads out of doors or windows, watching the action unfold. There were third-floor balconies brimming with gawkers. Clearly, they wanted to see what the outsider was made of.

As Hannah tossed and tussled and took down her adversaries, she noticed one Blue Scarf not getting in on the action. A short woman with long dark hair stood just outside the circle, watching Hannah with an unwavering gaze. Something about her felt familiar, but Hannah was too busy to figure it out.

Hannah ducked as a hand like a knife lashed out at her. She had had about enough of this hand-to-hand stuff; it was time to get serious.

Her eyes flashed red, and with a flurry of controlled ice

blasts, she began to trap those attacking her. Within seconds, the Blue Scarves became grotesque ice sculptures, straining to break free of their frozen restraints.

But the fight wasn't over. A cry sounded from above, and Hannah saw one of the balconies starting to topple. A dozen Solyrians held on tightly, preparing for the fall. Hannah sprinted. One of the wooden stilts supporting the balcony had been neatly severed, and the whole structure threatened to collapse.

Hannah grabbed one of the beams and channeled her magic into it, converting the old wood to hardened steel. Then she ran to another, and another. Within seconds, the structure had been supported enough that not only would it not fall now, it would likely outlast the rest of the block.

She turned back toward the Blue Scarves, but they were gone, shattered ice all that remained.

"Screw this," Hannah exclaimed as she took off in a sprint. "You're not getting away from me."

The city was a dense, maze-like configuration of buildings and alleys. Even with all the strength and speed at her disposal, she might have gotten lost. But Hannah had more than magic. She had know-how. Experience. She had been born and raised in a place like this and had fought tooth and nail to survive in a place like this.

Solyr wouldn't get the best of her.

Letting her instincts guide her as much as her senses, Hannah tore through the town, racing past startled citizens. It didn't take her long to catch a glimpse of her escaping prey. Even among a force as well-trained as the Blue Scarves, there was always a weak link.

Two of the Blue Scarves, a large lumbering man and an equally sizable woman, were apparently not as adept at hide and seek as the others. Hannah caught up with the pair as they tried to pull each other over a high wall at the back of a garbage-filled alley. Hannah used her magic to hurl the remains of a discarded rope at the woman. It coiled around her leg and pulled her to the ground. The giant man turned with a snarl on his face and charged Hannah. He looked like he could have tackled a statue without breaking stride.

Hannah simply sidestepped him at the last moment, and with a push of her hand, she converted his attack into a ground-shaking fall. But before Hannah could seal the deal, she caught a boot to the face.

The kick was hard, and Hannah stumbled back. She looked up at the new source of attack to find the young woman who had stayed out of the fight. She stood, fists at the ready. "Get out of here," she shouted, and the giants obeyed.

"You can't beat me," Hannah stated plainly.

The woman responded with her fists. Unlike the other Mylek, she didn't show any outward manifestation of her body magic except for the yellow eyes, yet she moved like she was made for fighting. Fast, fluid attacks followed one after another without an obvious pattern, nearly outpacing Hannah's speed. If it wasn't for Karl's training, she might have been taken down by this young woman.

Hannah couldn't help but be impressed.

She needed answers, and that required winning this fight.

Hannah ducked a high kick and placed her palms on

the ground. A thick root burst through the cobblestone street, wrapping itself around the Blue Scarf's waist. She clawed at it, nearly shredding the root, but it didn't matter. The root was no more than a distraction. Hannah found the rope again and pulled it toward her, coiling it around the woman's shoulders and arms.

Beneath the blue scarf, Hannah could see her yellow eyes widen in alarm.

"It's over," Hannah said. "I told you you couldn't beat me."

"No," the woman responded. "But my people escaped. That's what matters. You'll never find them now."

Hannah reached up and pulled the woman's mask off, and once again, she thought she looked familiar. A young girl, barely out of her teens if Hannah guessed right, with dark hair.

"I saw you," Hannah finally said. "The first day I arrived. You were part of the mob. Why are you doing all this?"

The young woman shook her head. "You'd never understand. You're just like them."

"Try me," Hannah said. "I'm here to help."

The woman looked at her as if she were calculating how to respond, but before she got the chance, she took a short club to the head.

"Hey!" Hannah turned to see a smiling Irmand with club in hand. "I had it under control, you freaking ogre."

"And we thank you," Irmand said, "but we've got it from here."

A dozen of his men quickly surrounded the young woman, gripping her tightly as they lifted her from the ground and locked her in chains. She tried to struggle, but one of the guards sent a calloused fist into her stomach.

"Take it easy," Hannah said, but Irmand just smirked.

"You did your part. This is city business now. This little shit has been tearing this city apart, but now the city is going to get some justice."

CHAPTER THIRTY-ONE

"Incoming," Aysa yelled as she snatched the knife out of thin air. She looked at its point, her eyes tracing the sharp blade. It was not a weapon of war, but common cutlery. She glanced over Parker with a tipsy giggle. "Want to play?"

Before he could answer, she flipped the knife over in her hand, grabbed it by the blade, and threw it thirty yards across the dining hall toward Karl, who stood up against the wall. He raised his mug, and the blade sank an eighth of an inch into the wooden stein.

"Drink, ye rat bastard," Karl shouted across the room.

A crowd had formed around them, and they all cheered as Aysa tilted the bottom of her mug toward the vaulted ceiling. It was a party like none Parker had seen for weeks, if not months.

The entire place was alive with energy. As far as Parker knew, the people of Solyr were preparing for the funeral party, but apparently, all of the provisions that had been brought into the city for King Aurel's final resting day had been diverted to this celebration. A celebration of the demise of the Blue Scarves, or at least their leader's capture.

"Well?" Aysa asked with a bit of a slur.

Parker shook his head and laughed. "I know better than to mess with the rearick and the girl from Baseek in a drinking game, especially one that includes weapons."

"It's not a weapon," Aysa shot back. Her brow furrowed. "It's just a steak knife."

Parker grinned. "Close enough. How's this work?"

"Comin' at ye!" Karl shouted from across the room. Parker watched the knife fly at them, end over end. Aysa shifted to her left, and the knife sank deep into the wall behind her.

"Drink, short stuff." She wrenched the knife out of the wall and took three paces toward Karl. She inspected the blade's point to make sure it could still bite flesh if necessary. "It's easy. You'd be good at it—for a round or two. All you have to do is throw the knife, and if you miss your opponent, you get to drink."

Parker shook his head. "I can't believe I'm actually on your team."

Aysa tilted her head to the side. "It's better than being on the other team, right?" She turned her eyes back toward Karl. "Knives up!" She threw the blade, and Karl struck it out of the air with a silver food platter. The crowd roared again.

"I expect you two will be super drunk before you get close to drawing first blood."

"That's what makes it fun." Aysa laughed. "Sure you don't want to play?"

"I think I'll go check on Hannah."

Aysa waved her hand. "Drinking and throwing sharp objects is way more fun than making out. Believe me, I've tried both."

Parker was still laughing as he walked across the hall. Aysa was one of a kind; the only person who might actually be more out there was Karl. He and Hannah had come a long way since the Boulevard in Arcadia, and Parker had to admit he didn't mind this life or his companions. Sure, he missed the rest of the crew, especially Hadley, even though he'd never tell the mystic that. But if you had to have anybody on the team to keep things interesting, it would be the rearick and the Baseeki.

Weaving through the crowd, he could almost taste the excitement amongst them. The Blue Scarves had been causing disruption in their society for too long. As far as Irmand and the others were concerned, they were probably the ones who had assassinated their beloved king.

Parker thought of Vitali and his information-gathering mission and scanned the crowd, looking for the Lynqi, but he was nowhere in sight. However, Parker did get a line of sight on a beautiful young woman standing alone with a drink across the room. He wondered if he could get her attention for a few minutes.

He beelined it for Hannah, a few people stopping him along the way, congratulating him on the work he and the rest of the team had done to save the city, both at the burning apartment and on the streets with the steers. Each of them, though, really wanted to talk about Hannah. As usual, she was the one on everyone's mind, Parker's included.

After the tenth person stopped him, he excused himself and cut across the room with his eyes on the floor, hoping he could make it across.

"You come here often?" Parker said with his shoulders pushed back.

"Not often enough," Hannah replied. "I never thought I'd find a guy like you in a place like this."

"Is that a good thing?" Parker asked, his face screwed up in confusion.

"I guess you could say it's open for interpretation." She smiled. "It can mean whatever you want it to mean."

"All right. I think it means that you want to get out of this place and settle down in that five-star apartment they gave you."

Hannah raised an eyebrow and twisted a spoon in her drink. Lifting the glass to her lips, she tilted it and took a sip.

"What are you drinking?" Parker asked.

"I've got no idea, but it is bloody delightful. I could drink these all night. Fruity, like raspberry, with a bite at the end."

Parker raised his hand to her cheek. "Given the blush you have right now, I'd say you probably *have* been drinking these all night."

Hannah laughed. He could tell she was loosening up, which at this point in the trip was a good thing for all of them. "I love to see you smile like that."

"Like what?"

"I don't know. I guess like you mean it. We've been grinding it out on the road for so long, and every minute since we landed here. A real smile looks good on you."

Hannah took another step in and looked up at Parker, her eyes dancing around his face. "You look good, too. Maybe someday we can do this more often."

"Yeah," Parker replied. "Maybe someday, we'll find a place like this of our own. But for now..."

Hannah nodded, and a shade of seriousness flashed across her face for a moment. "Yeah, for now, we need to figure out what the hell's going on here. This is not over. I'm sure of that."

Parker waved at a young man who was walking around with a tray of hors d'oeuvres. He came over, and Parker smiled at him. He was clearly Mylek, serving the Myrna royalty and their guests. He grabbed the small savory dish, some sort of mushroom wrapped in meat from one of the steers, and popped it in his mouth. "Thank you," he said with the sincerest smile he could muster. The servant nodded, bowed a little, and walked away.

"I know it's not over. I get the strange sense that things aren't as they seem. Today was too easy. I mean, I know you're a bad-ass replica of the Queen Bitch, but things went a little too swimmingly.

Hannah laughed. "Yeah. Things going according to plan isn't really our MO."

"Not even close," Parker agreed.

"Do you mind if I join the guest of honor?" Irmand asked, walking toward them. He spoke with a lilt, and his eyes danced in celebration of the major victory.

Parker held his tongue instead of telling the captain of

the guard to leave them the hell alone for a few more minutes.

"Of course, Captain Irmand," Hannah replied. "It is an honor."

Parker could barely stifle a laugh in response to his girlfriend's words. She had come a long way since her days in the Boulevard when she was young, brash, and smart-mouthed. Diplomatic would've never been a word used to describe her, and that was just what she was being right now. She had grown up; he guessed they both had, in their own way.

"The honor is all mine," Irmand told her. "Believe me, when I saw you fighting, and when your crew saved our town from the fire, it was like the Matriarch had landed in our little city to right what was wrong. You are like the Queen Bitch incarnate."

Hannah's face turned pink. Even though she had heard these words from others from time to time, they still struck her. Half the reason for her reaction was that she knew Irmand was more right than he suspected. With the Matriarch's blood running through Hannah's veins, she was nearly unstoppable. If they hadn't grown up together since birth, Parker would be more than a little intimidated by her.

"Well, let's not go overboard," Hannah answered. "We're just doing our job."

Irmand nodded as if his head were on a spring. "Well, your job saved our asses. And for that, I'm grateful." He waved toward the celebration in the hall and smiled. "And to show you our thanks, we give you all this."

Parker and Hannah looked out over the crowd and took in the "better half" of the city dancing, eating, drinking, and carrying on. Kirill had spared no expense for the celebration. The group was certainly pleased, no matter whose honor it was in, but he couldn't help but notice that the place was full of Myrna nobles. The only Mylek in the vicinity were the ones serving the food.

It felt like Arcadia. Parker saw that Hannah felt it too.

Diplomacy reigned once again. Mostly. "Well, I hope that at some point, the entire city will get to celebrate the victory."

Irmand looked at his feet and then back at her. His eyes still danced, but a little less. "Yes. Yes, I understand. Our city has had its share of division. King Aurel was working to heal wounds that go back generations. The unrest dates to the end of the Madness. But these things take time, and once Kirill takes the throne, his regime will finally bring about peace."

"Aren't you forgetting something?" Parker asked. "He has to win the election first."

"Yes, of course." Irmand nodded. "He does indeed, even though everyone knows Aurel planned to nominate Kirill as his successor and would have if not for his untimely death. Still, we will follow the city's charter, and if justice has its way, the process will yield the proper heir. I'm not concerned about that. And with that Blue Scarf troublemaker in custody, this town can relax."

Hannah took a sip from her drink, then said, "What can you tell me about her?"

A look of anger passed over Irmand's face. "Not much.

Her name is Aliz; we managed to wrangle that out of her, at least. But there's little more we need to know. She's a terrorist, and Solyr has ways of dealing with those who threaten our peace. I'd like to think the Patriarch would smile upon our land and laws. Now that she's under lock and key, we can force her to tell us where her compatriots are hiding. Then we'll deal with the rest of the Mylek…I mean, Blue Scarf scum."

Irmand's eyes cut between Hannah and Parker. He was clearly trying to read their reaction. Perhaps he trusted them as far as they trusted him. Raising his glass, he thanked them again. "To your Brigade and to our city. May they journey ever forward in the grace of the Matriarch."

Hannah tapped his glass with hers and smiled. "Ever forward."

Irmand ambled off, and Karl, clearly half in the bag, stumbled up to take his place. "What's that asshat doin' now?"

Parker looked him up and down. Karl wasn't bleeding, and Parker could only assume Aysa had also made it through their drinking game unscathed.

"They're gonna torture the girl. That's what they're up to," Hannah spat.

"You don't approve?" Parker asked.

"I didn't like it when you were tortured," she snarled. Parker nodded. He remembered clearly his time at the mercy of Adrien's minions.

Karl took a long draw from his mug and wiped his mouth with the back of his hand. "That's not entirely the same thing. That girl, as ye call her, did burn down the largest buildin' in town and let loose them steers to finish off the job."

"No one died," Hannah answered.

"Aye, they didn't. But that could be because the BBB was here. How many lives would've been lost if not fer us? If not fer you. I fer one have learned not to underestimate the power of girls." He gave her a wink.

"And furthermore—" Karl stopped short and grabbed his shoulder, a knife protruded between his fingers. "Son of a bloody mother-lovin' Baseeki rat-bastard." His eyes swept around the room. "Speakin' of girls!"

"I win." Aysa laughed from across the hall.

"Ye cheated!" Karl pulled the knife out of his shoulder and took off after his greatest adversary.

Parker laughed as Karl ran after Aysa. When he turned back to Hannah, he could tell she wasn't in a laughing mood.

"You think I'm taking all this with Irmand a little too seriously?" she asked.

"Seriously?" he asked. "In our line of work, a little suspicion goes a long way. When was the last time anyone in a position called 'Captain of the Guard' was totally on the up and up?"

"Why is that?" She sighed into her cup. "Is it too much to ask for nobility without douche-nuggetry?"

"Probably." Parker sighed. "Does power corrupt the thirsty, or do the powerful thirst for corruption?"

Hannah smiled. "Whoa. He's dashing *and* philosophical."

"What can I say?"

"A lot. You generally say a lot." She laughed.

"Me?" He gave her a feigned look of offense. "Anyway, I don't know what to say about Aliz, but Irmand does make me uncomfortable."

"Yeah. How so?"

"Well, again, whenever anybody is excited about justice—I mean his kind of justice—I automatically get very nervous."

Hannah nodded. "Almost reminds me of Andre McCocksmear back in the Boulevard."

"Bloody hell! I almost forgot about old Andre Assface."

Andre was one of the Hunters back in the Boulevard. His taste for dishing out pain exceeded his desire for justice. He was a sick, twisted man, and that sickness spread through the ranks of the other guards in Arcadia.

Something Hannah and Parker had put an end to with their revolution.

"It felt pretty good to take that one down, didn't it?" Parker grinned.

"Taking any of those guard bastards down felt good, but some felt better than others, including Andre O'Dicknose."

She looked around the room, and Parker could see she was trying to figure out the angle. Sure, the balance of power was clearly tipped against the Mylek. But for the most part, the Myrna certainly did not seem like a despicable bunch.

She turned back to Parker and handed him her glass. "Hold this for me."

"Where you going?"

Hannah nodded at the crowd. "I'm going to get some answers. When everything seems right but our gut says it's wrong, we trust our gut."

"Damn straight," Parker said. He took her glass, looked down at it, and then back up at her. "I've got a feeling you're not coming back for this."

Hannah went up on her tiptoes and gave him a kiss on the lips. "Maybe. Maybe not. Don't wait up for me, okay, dear?"

CHAPTER THIRTY-TWO

Hannah smiled as wide as she could as she wove through the crowd. She knew everyone was excited about the capture of Aliz and what seemed to be the total deconstruction of the Blue Scarves, but the attention made her more than a little uncomfortable.

Unlike her assistance in most cities, Irmand and Kirill and their people were more than happy to give credit where credit was due. Hannah was a damn celebrity, but at that moment, she wanted nothing more than to blend in with the crowd. It took her nearly fifteen minutes to cross the room, but when she got there, she found exactly who she was looking for sitting in a corner.

"You still on the lam?" Hannah asked.

"I might be." Vitali smiled. "I don't know what that means. Is it something that your people say in the west? We surely don't say that in Kaskara."

Hannah smiled and reached toward her friend. Placing her hand on his shoulder, she gave it a squeeze and said,

"It's good to see you, Vitali. You missed some major fireworks."

He nodded. "It's all anyone can talk about. Besides you, of course."

She shrugged. "What can I say, they like me. So, why are you over here in his dark corner?"

Vitali spread his hands across the linen table and looked around the room. "You could say I'm still keeping an eye on the place, which would be true. But I also got asked for drinks three times by a couple of rich pricks."

"That kinda sucks," Hannah said.

"Yeah. And there are like a half-dozen Myrna women who asked me if I would mind them touching my fur."

Hannah laughed. "That really sucks. But to be fair, when I was hanging out with your people out east, there were no fewer than a dozen Lynqi who asked if they could touch my bare skin."

"That's because your bare skin makes no sense. But I assume you didn't come over here to discuss differences and social conventions."

"No, I most certainly did not. I need your advice."

Vitali nodded, and Hannah could swear she heard a purr emanating from his chest. Vitali didn't mind working alone, but his people were also communal. Hannah could only assume that just being together gave him a sense of peace, a moment of happiness. Being with him made her content too.

"I'm happy to help."

"It's just that none of this makes sense," she began. "At least, not given the information I have. I feel like we're intentionally being kept in the dark."

"And you don't like being in the dark," Vitali added.

"Bingo-bango. What do you know?"

"Not much that would shed light, unfortunately. I don't love Kirill. He's all smiles, but there are sharp teeth behind it. I don't doubt he would do nasty things to gain power."

"Like kill his father?"

Vitali thought for a second. "I don't know. There were no marks on the body, so Aurel could have been killed by a magic user."

"That would mean a Myrna," Hannah mused. "Like Kirill."

"Him, or half the city. Or maybe I'm wrong."

"Doesn't really narrow things down, does it?" Hannah tapped her foot, thinking about the next move.

"I'm sorry," Vitali said. "What about on your end?"

"Not much." Hannah sighed. "I didn't get much of a chance to talk to the Blue Scarf girl, Aliz, before Irmand's men jumped her. She was not happy, but like you said, there's a ton of unhappy people around here. With all that considered, what should we do?" Hannah asked, knowing exactly what Vitali was going to say.

"We talk to people who aren't happy." Vitali held up a finger and pointed at a woman in a long black cocktail dress. "How about her? I've been watching her all night, and she certainly doesn't seem to be in a partying mood."

Hannah followed his eyes to see the woman they had met on their first day in town. She was a Mylek on the city council.

Hannah rose. "Good call, V. And listen, since you don't seem to be enjoying the party either…"

"You would like me to keep investigating?"

"Yep. Someone in this city has to know something about the dead king. Somebody who might talk."

Vitali smiled. "I have the perfect person in mind."

"Good," Hannah smiled. "And be careful, will you?"

Vitali nodded. "Nothing you wouldn't do."

He nodded again, then disappeared around the corner.

"That doesn't fill me with confidence," she shouted to him. But he was already gone.

Hannah moved quickly toward her mark, brushing off the smiling crowd. She was done playing the humble savior. She needed answers.

The woman was beautiful by all social standards. Tall, fit, with long, flowing amber hair that fell below her shoulders. Her eyes sparkled, and Hannah assumed she looked ten years younger than her actual age. Nevertheless, she wasn't on the A-List here.

She was a Mylek, after all.

"This is one hell of a party," Hannah said as she stood eye to eye with the woman.

"Nothing gets this city more excited than a bad guy being put behind bars."

Hannah smiled. "You mean, bad girl?"

The woman smiled back. "If we're going to be precise, I prefer 'bad woman.' But I won't diddle over words with you." She shoved her hand toward Hannah, and Hannah took it in her own. "I'm Ky."

Hannah nodded. "I remember. We met when I first

came here. It feels like a month ago, but it's only been days."

"Time certainly bends when things go sideways. I guess I should thank you for all that you've done to straighten things out. The fire. The stampede."

Hannah couldn't help but notice that she left out the Blue Scarves.

"It's what we do," Hannah said. "Hopefully, Irmand can keep the peace from here on out."

The woman nodded. "The peace. Right. Although I don't know who writes his job description these days."

Hannah's face must have shown her shock because Ky hurriedly continued,

"The captain of the guard is not a bad person. I know you heard me dress him down in front of the council, but I've known Irmand since we were kids. He's a good man. Good intentions. Totally inadequate for the job at hand, but I imagine that's why he was hired."

"Really?" Hannah said. "What do you mean?"

Ky shrugged. "There's not much more to say. Maybe a bit of chaos is helpful to some people in Solyr. And although Kirill would not agree, I'm loyal to this place. To these people. Even to poor Irmand, who keeps tripping over his dick."

Hannah couldn't help but laugh at Ky's vulgarity. "Can I ask you another question? Frankly?"

"I'm nothing if not frank."

"Good. What do you know about Aliz?" Hannah asked.

Ky shook her head. "Just because I'm a Mylek, you expect me to know every other Mylek in this city? Thousands of us live here."

"That's not an answer," Hannah shot back, her voice harsher than she intended.

"No, I suppose it isn't." The woman smiled. "Forgive me; it's been one hell of a long day."

"And yet you're not celebrating," Hannah pushed.

"You won't find many Mylek who are."

Ky took a long drink from her glass. After placing it on a high table next to her, she looked at Hannah and said, "I'm happy you caught that woman. Truly, I am. The chaos the Blue Scarves were spreading in our city was terrible, but I can't help but fear what comes next. From where I sit, this is just another brick in the wall Kirill and his minions are building between the Mylek and power.

"I can understand why the young people are frustrated. Things aren't great for us, and it wasn't long ago that things were even worse. King Aurel was, at least for us Mylek, a good king. He understood us, even though he wasn't one of us. That was why he put me on the council. He's why I'm here. He wanted me to represent my people. And there were some of us…"

She fell silent. Hannah placed her hand on Ky's shoulder. "What?"

"Hope is a dangerous thing," Ky said. "And some of the Mylek hoped one of us would find the throne next. But Aurel died, and now that Irmand has his big bad Mylek monster behind bars, Kirill's victory is all but assured. But at least we have the villain, right? At least we have peace."

Ky grabbed her drink off the table and walked away. Hannah's head swam. She could feel the emotion of the woman, and she empathized with her. Things were very different between Solyr and Arcadia, and things were more subtle here. Subtleties made things much more insidious. Which meant she would have to be all the more obstinate.

Hannah realized it was time to talk to their villain.

CHAPTER THIRTY-THREE

Karl dropped the bottle of ale by his side and let out a rumbling belch loud enough to make Sal raise his head, ready to fight whatever treacherous monster was approaching. "Take 'er easy, ol' guy," Karl said, giving him a rub on the neck. "It's just nature gettin' the best of me."

"Speaking of things getting the best of you, how's your shoulder, rearick?" Aysa laughed.

Karl put his palm against his shoulder and felt a tiny biting sting from where she had hit him with a steak knife. "It's nothin', kid. But I'll grant ye, that was one helluva throw. Especially for a drunk-ass Baseeki like yerself."

"Wait until your drunk wears off. It will scream at you tomorrow morning." Aysa stood and steadied herself. "Some of us have extreme self-control even when we drink. It's one of my special talents."

Karl snorted. "Bullshit. Ye couldn't brush yer teeth right now if ye needed to. Even if ye had two good hands."

"I could do almost anything right now," the girl slurred. "Blindfolded."

"Sure. Whatever. Wonder if ye could find another bottle or two of ale."

Aysa ignored his call for more booze. "For instance, I could certainly kick your ass right now."

Karl waved her off. The last thing he wanted to do when he was half in the bag was mess around with the one-handed warrior.

"Or I could fix the *Unlawful* right now."

"Like hell, ye could. Ye can hardly see straight."

Aysa closed one eye and squinted the other. "Pretty straight. Like this, at least. Let's go. I'll prove it."

Karl exhaled and looked toward the residences. He certainly didn't want to go all the way back there to retrieve the mechanism they'd bought in town. One look at his feather bed and he'd be going nowhere except Sleepville, and fast.

It was like the girl could read his mind. She patted her backpack and smiled. "I've got all I need right here, old man. Didn't let it leave my sight."

Karl had a feeling she wasn't going to let this one go. "I'll take ye up on that bet. Ye fix that machine, and I'll take a week's worth of yer chores on our voyage out of this place."

"And if I don't?" Aysa asked.

"*When* you don't, ye need to take a vow of silence for a week. Not one bloody word." Karl grinned at his friend. "What do ye think?"

"No words for a week? Not a problem."

"I've never heard ye be quiet fer a minute, let alone an hour," Karl said.

"Not a problem, because I'm gonna nail this. Let's go."

There was a little more than a mile to where they had parked the *Unlawful* up in the clouds, and Sal got them there in a few minutes. That was Aysa's idea. She loved riding the dragon, and even more, she loved how uncomfortable it made Karl. The rearick held onto the dragon's neck, while Aysa sat behind him whooping and hollering all the way. Her head spun, the buzz from the ale mixing with the exhilaration of flight.

"Can't wait till that damn trap of yers is shut," Karl grumbled under his breath. Aysa laughed harder. She knew he only half-meant it.

When they hit the ground, Aysa pulled the black remote out of her bag and pressed the button. She could hear the gentle whir of the core kicking energy into the ship's engines from where they stood.

As the ship powered down, the hum of the engine was replaced by a different sound. Loud shouts echoed in chorus from the hills above them.

"Looks like we've got company," Karl shouted as he raised his hammer to the ready.

"Now, this is a party," Aysa said. Her shield was already strapped to her arm, and she had a set of bolas in hand. She recognized the attackers within seconds. "Bloody pirates. I barely got a chance to fight them last time."

"Well, it's yer lucky night. Looks like they been lyin' in wait for us." He pointed his hammer toward a small group, maybe twenty, sprinting down the hill toward them.

"Bad idea." Aysa laughed as she tossed her first pair of bolas. The weapon wrapped around a charging man's ankles, and as he collapsed to the dirt, two others tripped over him. She grabbed another pair from her belt and began swinging them over her head as she ran toward the force.

Two versus twenty would have been a tough fight even for warriors of Karl and Aysa's caliber, but they weren't fighting alone. Aysa blocked spears with her shield and Karl shattered them with his hammer, but Sal did most of the work. To their credit, the pirates didn't run in terror at the sight of the dragon, but courage meant very little against his claws and teeth and tail. Whatever semblance of order they had attacked in was torn to shreds by Sal's persistence dive-bombs.

Aysa cracked one of the pirates' skulls open with her bolas. "They didn't think this through very well."

Karl took out another's legs. "Aye. We'll finish with these in minutes and still have time to fix—"

Before he could finish, a loud roar filled the valley.

"This ship!" Aysa shouted. She turned around and saw the *Unlawful* begin to rise. She pulled the black remote from her pocket and jammed the button, but the device refused to listen.

"A diversion," Karl shouted as he knocked a spear aside, his voice suddenly more sober than it had sounded for hours. "Go, I'll handle things down here."

Aysa let loose her last pair of bolas at a pirate aiming for Karl's unguarded back, then took off at a sprint. Sal was right behind her. She pulled one of the short spears the pirates favored from the mud before jumping onto Sal's back. They soared after the rising wooden airship.

Apparently, the pirates had expected a fight in the sky.

Three pirates wearing those damned kites launched from the bow of the *Unlawful,* spears at the ready.

"Dead ahead, Sal," she shouted. She held on tight with her long legs and pointed her spear forward.

The cold wind stung her face, but she refused to blink. The distance between her and the pirates closed in seconds. Two broke off to flank them, but Aysa didn't take the bait. Her focus was on the lead. She held her shield high.

"Come at me, you bastard!" she shouted. Sal roared in unison.

She leaned into the attack, and with the advantage afforded by her long arms, she struck first. Her spear sank deep while the pirate's weapon shattered on her shield, and like that, the sky was clear. She watched as his lifeless body fluttered to the ground.

There was little time to revel in the victory. The two other flyers were coming at them.

"I need to secure the ship, Sal. Can you handle these two flying assholes?"

The dragon responded by flapping his powerful wings harder. Within seconds, they had crested the bow of the *Unlawful.* Aysa dropped to the wooden deck and Sal went after his prey. Aysa, armed only with her shield, turned her fist toward the door.

"It's time to take my freaking ship back."

CHAPTER THIRTY-FOUR

Karl raised his hammer and eyed the three remaining pirates. With Aysa and Sal gone, there was no one to watch his back, and he was quickly surrounded by spears, although none of them attacked.

"What are ye waitin' for, ye yellow-bellied bastards?" They didn't respond to his taunts. Instead, they stepped aside as a man at least a head taller than the rest of the pirates stepped out of the shadows. He held two small axes in his hands.

"Remember me, little man?"

"Aye," Karl said. "Happy to have a chance to keep me promise."

The man smiled. "We're on stable ground this time. Don't expect any tricks to save you."

"Well, quit yer blabberin' then if ye feel so damn confident."

The man charged, and once again, Karl was struck by the brute's speed. If it wasn't for the fact that Karl constantly trained with Parker and Vitali, the pirate's ferocity might have outdone him. Karl dodged as well as he fought, and he managed to jab his hammer into the man's stomach.

The pirate stumbled back. He must have been wearing armor under his loose-fitting dark clothing; otherwise, the hammer would have split his stomach open. As it was, Karl knew the hit would leave him pissing blood for a week.

"Aye, ye like that?" Karl laughed.

The pirate roared in anger, then leapt back into the fray. This time, his three spearmen joined in. Karl was good, but one against four were terrible odds for anyone, except maybe Hannah. He swung wide, trying to give himself as much space as possible, but these pirates were good with the spears, and with the hatchet-wielding maniac at the lead, they knew how to fight.

Karl barely managed to dodge an axe that cut his arm. Idly, he wondered how Aysa was fairing, but he knew better than to waste his energies fretting over that girl. She'd be just fine. Instead, he gritted his teeth and fought on.

He kept his feet and managed to keep the four fighters in front of him. That left his back safe, and his hammer was a mighty wall. He took a step back as the pirates held up for a second. "Come on then," Karl yelled. "Next one that steps forward loses his head."

They must have thought he meant it because they stood still. Karl laughed. "What's the matter? Afraid of this little man?"

The large pirate grabbed one of his men and threw him forward. Karl gripped his hammer and prepared to strike, but he never got a chance. A body fell from the sky and crushed the man into the ground.

Karl and the pirates stared in horror at the mangled bodies, then looked up. The rearick barely had a chance to jump aside before the *Unlawful* came crashing to the ground in an explosion of dirt.

The rearick picked himself up and brushed the dirt off. As the dust cleared, there was no sign of the pirates. Either they fled or found their deaths under the hull of the *Unlawful.*

"Hey, Karl," Aysa shouted from the deck. "Once you're done dicking around down there, I could use some help. I need to clean the blood and guts out of the engine room before I can fix it. That is, if our deal is still good."

"Aye." He laughed, his buzz barely coming back to him. "Our deal is still good. But I think I'm gonna need another drink first."

CHAPTER THIRTY-FIVE

Vitali lowered his hood and let cool wind sweep through his fur. It felt good to be outside after being cooped up in the royal chambers all day. Out here, there was little risk of his appearance offending anyone.

There was no one outside.

It was late when he left Kirill's party in the grand hall, but not so late as to justify the silent streets before him. The message among the elites was "Victory, the evil that terrorized our city has been defeated." But that message of the saviors had apparently failed to make much of an impact down here among the people who had supposedly been saved.

The king's murderer was still on the loose, after all.

They killed the king, the old Mylek woman had said. *Anyone powerful enough to do that could kill anyone they wanted.*

Vitali walked quickly, the cobblestones under his feet giving way to packed dirt, which gave way to mud as he moved farther from the city center. As the nice shops disappeared from view, they were replaced by establishments with dark windows and thick doors. He only had one lead left, but he was fairly confident in his intel.

If he wanted answers, this would be the kind of place to ask questions.

Vitali found the building he was looking for. It had no sign, no outward indication that it was open for business, but he could hear laughter and revelry inside.

Not everyone was afraid tonight. Vitali raised his hood and stepped through the doorway.

His eyes adjusted quickly to the dim light inside. An empty bar took up one side of the room, and the rest was filled with tables and soft-looking chairs. The place was packed with men and women enjoying the company of others. Every once in a while, a couple stood up and moved through a curtain in the back. They laughed loudly and held each other close as they went.

The central feature of this back-alley establishment was the utter lack of Mylek features. Everyone was clearly Myrna, born and bred. Everyone except Vitali. He pulled his hood tighter around his face and found a stool at the bar.

The bartender, a woman maybe twice Vitali's age, although he struggled to tell sometimes among the furless, slid a heavy glass mug toward him. His nose twitched at the smell.

"I didn't order anything yet," he told her.

"Didn't have to," she responded. "It's the only thing we serve. That and a little short-term company. But something tells me a man with his cloak wrapped that tightly around him isn't looking for company."

Vitali took a sip of the bitter liquid. "The people in this town seem more comfortable in my company when they can't see what's under the hood."

"Then the people you've met are assholes. You're one of them, aren't ya? The one's who've come to 'save us?'"

"Something like that," Vitali responded.

She grabbed a rag, cleaner than Vitali expected it to be, and wiped a glass before filling it. She raised it in his direction. "Then you're welcome here."

Vitali raised his drink in reply. "Thank you. It's nice to meet someone who isn't...an asshole."

She took a long drink, then turned to look at the curtain in the back. "Enjoy it while it lasts."

Vitali heard a loud laugh and twisted his head to follow the bartender's eyes. Emerging from the thick curtain was a massive man with a woman under each arm. He leaned heavily on them as he walked, and they seemed to strain under his weight.

Even though he wasn't wearing a uniform, he fit Thaed's description to a tee. From what Vitali had overheard while spying on Kirill, Thaed knew something about the king and his untimely death, which meant the Lynqi had come to the right place.

Vitali turned back toward his drink as the women deposited the customer at the bar.

He grunted. "Another drink."

"In a second," the bartender replied.

The large man fumbled in his pockets before pulling out a heavy metal coin. He slammed it down hard on the table. "Now."

She filled a glass and handed it to him, but when she

reached out to take the coin, his hand shot out like a whip and grabbed her wrist.

"I've got more where that came from, in case you were interested in stepping out from behind that bar."

She tried to pull away, but his grip was too tight. "Not my job, man."

He pulled her closer. "I said I've got the damn coin. I don't give a shit what your job is."

Vitali was on his feet and at the man's side in an instant. "Let her go," Vitali hissed.

Thaed turned his glassy eyes toward the Lynqi, not sure what he was seeing.

"Yeah? What's it to ya, then?" His voice was slurred with ire and drink.

"Nothing. Just sick of the assholes in this town."

Thaed let go of the bartender and stood. He was easily a head taller than Vitali, and twice as thick.

"Did you just call me an asshole?" He reached out to grab Vitali, but as he did, the small catman kicked Thaed's ankle. His leg buckled and he dropped to the ground hard, pulling his fresh mug of beer on top of him as he fell.

Everyone in the bar broke into laughter.

Thaed scrambled to his feet, his already-red cheeks turning redder. He looked like he wanted to scream or fight or burn the place down, but instead, he just ran out the door, the sound of laughter on his heels.

Vitali nodded to the bartender and followed the wet boot prints out the door.

CHAPTER THIRTY-SIX

Damp, dank air hung around her as Hannah descended into the lower chambers of the hold. She had managed to slip away from the party easily enough, and finding the prison was simply a matter of memory— Irmand's. She had seen it when she'd read his mind the first day he met her and her team, and she'd had him take them to the great hall instead.

Turning a corner, she found the guard station, which was empty. She could only assume Irmand had given his charges the night off for the celebration. It was, after all, they who should've been celebrated for the capture of Aliz.

As she proceeded down the hall, she found the reason Irmand was unconcerned about the guard post being vacant. Cells were lined up next to each other, secured with massive iron bars and locks with impossible-looking mechanisms. The prisoners weren't going anywhere. Hannah turned her hand over and her eyes lit up with the red of magic. A small blue orb floated in front of her, bringing light to the jailhouse. Drawn faces and sunken eyes looked out of each cell, all of them wordlessly begging for release. Hannah's heart beat in anticipation.

She couldn't help but wonder about the prisoners. Most of them were Mylek, although there were a few Myrna scattered among them. Were these violent terrorists like the Blue Scarves or products of Solyr's legal system? Maybe the two weren't so different. She half-considered melting the bars and breaking down the walls, but she decided to maintain discretion for the time being.

At least until she knew more.

But she swore she would bring Justice in due time.

"We will check on prisoner one and get back to the party," a familiar voice said from behind her.

Hannah extinguished her glowing orb and pressed her body against the wall. Irmand and one of his men came into sight. Her instincts told her to run, but Hannah wasn't the little girl from the Boulevard anymore. She sent a wave of magic into their minds, a suggestion that they saw nothing out of the ordinary, especially not a young woman trying to hide in plain sight.

Camouflaged by her mental magic, Hannah held her breath and listened.

"I'm sure she's secure, Captain, and it was clever of you to put her at the end of the hall, away from the others. I can't imagine she will be able to inspire a Blue Scarf revolution from behind bars."

Irmand shook his head. "Some of the most successful revolts began in chains."

Hannah held her breath and pushed further into Irmand's mind.

But the bloodiest of all revolutions come from foreigners inside the city, she suggested in the corners of his mind.

"We have nearly decimated the Blue Scarves revolution," the guard said.

Irmand nodded. "Yes, but sometimes, the bloodiest revolutions come from foreigners inside the city."

The young man by his side smiled. "The magician and her friends, then?"

Irmand's face lost all expression, and then he smiled broadly. "Indeed. We should get back to the great hall and keep watch."

As the footsteps of the captain of the guard and his trusted colleague faded back toward the stairwell, Hannah stepped away from the wall and walked toward the end of the hall. Prisoners looked up from several more cells, resigned to their place in the prison. Hannah could only imagine how these Mylek people might have tried to transform their bodies to escape the cells.

At the end of the corridor sat a single cell separated from the rest.

"You," Aliz said as Hannah stepped up to the bars.

She got off her cot and crossed the tiny room. The women stood eye to eye for a moment in silence. Hannah scanned her face. She was pretty, her features sharp and distinct. Her cheek was bruised on the left-hand side, indicating that she had taken more than one blow, probably from someone's fist. Hannah wondered if Irmand had already tried to pry information about the Blue Scarves and their plots out of her.

"Have you come to finish me off?" she asked.

"Depends," Hannah replied, "on what you've got to say."

"More torture, then?" the girl asked.

"Not my style. Just a conversation."

Aliz laughed. "The daughter of the Matriarch has a soft-spot? Not something I'd expect."

"Not one of the faithful?" Hannah dragged a chair over from the other side of the room. "Justice understands that there are three sides to every story."

"Three?" Aliz asked as she sat.

"Yes: yours, theirs, and what actually happened. I've heard what those holding the keys have to say. Now I want to hear from the one behind bars."

"What if I say no?"

Hannah shrugged. "Then you stay here, and I go back to the party. They have this one kick-ass dish. Little shrimpy thing on a toothpick. You know the one?"

Aliz kept her eyes on Hannah. There was strength in them. A fire burned inside her. Hannah took a second to dip into the woman's mind. As before, it was a storm of emotion, but in addition to the rage and fear, Hannah caught a hint of uncanny calmness in the shadows of the turmoil.

Hannah raised a hand to run over the headache forming behind her ear. "Last chance."

The girl sighed. "I'll talk to you. For whatever it's worth."

"I wouldn't be here if it was worth nothing," Hannah replied. She reached into her sling bag and pulled out a small flask. She pushed it through the bars toward Aliz. "A little something from the celebration to wet your whistle."

The girl smiled and looked sideways at the flask. "In the days before the Madness, there was a saying, 'Look a gift pig between the teeth.' Have you heard that one?"

Hannah tilted her head to the side. "I've heard a lot from the old days. Not that one. It's freaking weird, but I think I get your drift."

Aliz laughed a little and smiled. "Sure, it's weird, and helpful." She raised the flask toward Hannah. "But I think I'm going to choose to trust the giver, even though ancient wisdom advises against it. I've never been one to follow the old ways, and even if it is poison, I'm thirsty."

The girl closed her eyes and tilted the flask back, letting the sharp liquor bite her tongue. After a moment, she brought it down and pushed the flask back through the bars. "I sure hope that wasn't my last drink in Irth."

Hannah took the flask and gave the young woman a wink. "If it's yours, it's ours." She took her own drink slowly. Handing the flask back through the bars, she said, "The rest is yours. It's storytime."

Aliz laughed and took another sip, this one slower and more intentional. "It's good to drink from the court's store once again. It's been a long time for me, and I have seldom tasted liquor from the barrels beneath the great hall. Usually, I only drink the slop they serve down in the Flats."

"The Flats?"

"Yeah. It's where the Mylek hang out at night. Not a place you'd want your kids to go."

Hannah couldn't help but grin. "We have a similar place where I come from. They called it the Boulevard."

"So, you stayed away from there?"

She shook her head. "Was born and raised there."

"Maybe we're more alike than I expected." The young woman moved toward the wall and sat, then stretched her legs out in front of her and set the silver flask between them. "You've been here long enough to see what life is like for people like me."

"I have," Hannah agreed. "But I don't see how burning down buildings changes that."

"It didn't start that way. At first, we just wanted to make a statement, you know? Let the world know that we wouldn't be kicked to death quietly. We never meant to hurt anyone."

"You could have fooled me. What changed?"

Aliz took a long drink. "The king."

"From what I hear, Aurel was good for the Mylek."

"He was," Aliz said. "The best we had ever known. He put one of us on the council. Made some serious changes. For the first time ever, a system that had seemed etched in stone started to fade. We felt hope."

Hannah nodded, listening to the woman's story. "Having hope in a city of injustice is not such a bad thing."

"No." Aliz shrugged. "But it can be dangerous."

The way the young Mylek stared at Hannah, it was as if she knew Hannah's own story of hope.

"I guess it can," Hannah admitted.

"And it wasn't just the Mylek who felt that way. Plenty of Myrna resisted the king's changes. Like his asshole son."

"Kirill." Hannah grimaced. "I thought he worshiped his dad."

Aliz laughed. "Maybe to his face, but just look at how

things have changed since Aurel's death. Kirill is already trying to beef up his control of the guard. Irmand and his assholes can basically do whatever they want. He's raised taxes on the Mylek, and instead of using that money to help the city, he's filling his war chest."

She paused and studied Hannah's face before continuing. "The prince only cares about one thing, which is power. He hated the fact that his dad was weakening the throne, and before his dad was cold, he started reversing those decisions. Before long, we'll lose every right we have. That's why the Blue Scarves did what we did. We have to show the Mylek that they're strong. Strong enough to fight back. Can you understand that?"

Hannah could understand that, all too well. But something held her back from believing fully. "You're awfully young to be a revolutionary."

Aliz shrugged. "I don't know. My mother died when I was young. My father couldn't care less about me. Basically, I have no family, so fighting and dying to make things better sounds like a good exchange to me. I guess it's easy when you've got little to lose."

"Everyone has something to lose."

"Not me." Aliz sighed. "All hope I had in a better life died when Aurel did. There was talk that maybe he'd appoint someone other than Kirill to the throne, but that was just another hope dashed. Kirill will win, and then we will all lose."

Hannah let the woman sit there and drink from the flask. Her words were slow and measured. Careful. Hannah couldn't help but wonder if Aliz thought Hannah was still her enemy. She dipped into the woman's mind again and found that it was, for the first time, at peace. Fully calm. Trusting. Maybe it was the alcohol running through her veins. It was, after all, why Hannah had brought it in the first place. She rubbed her headache again, wishing she had saved more of that drink for herself.

Finally, Hannah rose to her feet.

"Storytime is over?" Aliz asked. "What comes next?"

"I don't know." Hannah stared down at the girl. She seemed so fragile. "Listen, I promised this city I would do what I can to help, and I meant it. We're going to find Aurel's murderer, and we're going to try to set things right. I don't know where that leaves you. As powerful as I am, I don't have the power to forgive what you did and the people you hurt. But I understand, and I'll try to make sure the ones holding the keys understand too. Just give me some time."

Aliz tilted back the flask and finished its contents, then tossed it between the bars and started to laugh. "You make one hell of a speech, you know that? Unfortunately, your time is almost up. Once Kirill is elected, it won't matter what evidence you might find. He'll be in complete control, and Kirill will destroy everything good—starting with us."

CHAPTER THIRTY-SEVEN

The Lynqi are hunters born and raised, the bounty of the Kaskaran jungle providing more than enough for the cat-people's survival. Vitali could track a goat through the mountain cliffs. He could pluck a wild turkey before it even noticed he was there. He could take down a tiger with his paws.

But even if he was a blindfolded remnant, following Thaed would have been easy.

The large soldier stumbled drunkenly through the streets, mumbling loudly to himself as he went. Vitali could smell the old sweat and cheap booze rolling off the man from two blocks back.

Thaed seemed to have no clear direction. His drunken wandering was taking them on a meandering path through the city, but before long, a new scent filled Vitali's senses.

Burnt wood.

The large building smoldered in the night. Hannah and the others had prevented most of it from collapsing, but it would take months of work for the building to be habitable again.

Which made it the perfect location for Vitali to do his work.

He pulled his hood more tightly around his face and sprinted for the building. He slowed to a walk as he turned the corner, Thaed in his sights.

He moved slowly toward him.

"Excuse me," Vitali said, his voice low. "I was wondering if you could give me directions. I appear to be lost."

"What?" Thaed hadn't even noticed Vitali approaching. "Fuck off, ya wanker."

Vitali stepped closer and put his hand on the man's shoulder. "That's not very kind, friend. I heard that this city was known for its hospitality."

Thaed knocked Vitali's paw aside. "I said, get the hell away from me." He tried to walk past, but Vitali shifted to stay in front of him.

"Please. It will only take a minute."

"It will take less time than that for me to knock you on your ass." The drunk man's words came out slow and slurred. He swayed from one foot to the other as his eyes flashed black, and Vitali prepared for the magic that was about to follow, but nothing happened. Thaed stared at his empty hands.

"Trouble getting it up?" Vitali laughed. "I heard that can happen if you drink too much."

Thaed yelled, then balled up his large fist and swung. Vitali leaned back as it sailed by. The man stared, dumbfounded.

"How'd you do that?"

"If you think that's impressive," Vitali smiled, "wait until you see this."

He jumped, planting one foot on the man's chest and using the other to kick skyward as he flipped around. Vitali landed in a silent crouch and watched the lumbering man fall rigid to the ground. A second later, his snores filled the alley.

Vitali stalked around the unconscious man, wondering how to proceed. It seemed the nice approach wasn't working. Time to try something a bit more Hannah-like.

Carrying Thaed up the stairs, finding a chair stable enough to support his weight, and tying him to it was easier than what came next.

Vitali had to wake him up.

Whether due to the amount of booze swimming through the man's veins, or perhaps because Vitali had kicked him harder than he'd planned, Thaed was out cold. His snores echoed throughout the burnt shell of the building. Vitali shouted and slapped the man, to no avail. Then he found a bucket half-full of rainwater and dumped it on Thaed's head.

That did the trick.

"The hell is going on here?" he growled

"What's going on," Vitali said quietly from the shadows, "is that I'm going to ask you a few questions, and you're going to answer."

Thaed tried to lunge at him, but the ropes and the chair held.

"I'm goin' to rip your arms off, ya dumb bastard."

Vitali stepped into a beam of moonlight that shone into the burned-out building. He reached up and slowly lowered his hood.

"What the fu—"

Before Thaed could finish, Vitali shoved the man's chest. The chair tipped backward and started to fall through the hole in the floor, a hole that led to a three-story drop.

Before Thaed could plummet headfirst to the ground floor, Vitali grabbed a rope that hung from a sturdy beam in the ceiling down to Thaed's chair. He held tight, keeping the drunken man suspended upside-down over the gap.

"Shit shit shit shit shit," the Myrna cried over and over, like a prayer that might save his hide.

Vitali pulled down on the rope, lifting Thaed back into a sitting position. His curses gave way to whimpers.

"What do ya want?" Thaed sniveled, clearly aware that he was on the edge of mortal danger.

"I told you," Vitali growled, placing his paws on the man's legs, talons fully extended, and squeezing. "I need information. Tell me about Aurel."

The Lynqi didn't know what to expect since he wasn't used to this style of operating. Having Thaed burst into tears was definitely not part of the plan.

Vitali stood up and stared at the blubbering mess.

"The king, he was a good man," Thaed said with a sniffle. "He always seemed to know how I was feelin', and he knew the right words to cheer me up. What kind of king does that? I was his personal guard. I protected him for ten fuckin' years, but I couldn't save him. *I couldn't save him.*"

Vitali jumped in with a question before Thaed's sobs overtook him. "What happened that night? What were you doing outside the great hall so late?"

Thaed sat up straighter. "I can't say. I swore I'd keep my damned mouth shut."

Vitali fought the urge to pace. He considered tipping him over again, but he was no good at playing Hannah. Besides, the broken man in front of him just might shatter.

He decided to try the nice method again.

Vitali crouched in front of him. "Do you know who I am?"

Thaed nodded but wouldn't look at him.

"Do you know why I'm here?"

"You're with her," he finally stated.

"That's right," Vitali answered. "And we're here to help. I'm trying to find Justice for your king, to find out what happened to him. You can help me do that. You can help me stop your king's killers. Doesn't Aurel deserve that?"

Thaed nodded again, but this time, he met Vitali's eyes. Then he took a deep breath and told his story.

"Like I said, the king was a good man, but even good men deserve some...indiscretions. Aurel liked women." He raised a brow. "I mean, who doesn't?"

"He had a mistress?" Vitali clarified.

"Yeah. At least, that was what I always figured. He never introduced me, but I took him to the same house every night without fail. He would bring these nicely wrapped gifts along. Always insisted on carryin' them himself. I'd stand guard for a couple hours, and then we'd return to the great hall."

"Who was in that house?" Vitali asked, trying to hide

the desperation in his voice. Hannah needed these answers. The city needed answers.

Thaed shrugged. "Don't know. Only time I ever went in was the night he died. I heard a scream, busted down the door, and found him covered in blood."

Covered in blood, Vitali thought, *but he didn't have any external wounds.*

Thaed's tears startled Vitali from his thoughts.

"Hey," Vitali shouted. "There will be time to mourn later. Who else knew about this? About Aurel's late-night visits?"

"No one," Thaed said. "I was the only guard to ever go with him, and Aurel swore me to secrecy."

"Not Kirill? Not Irmand?"

"Are you shittin' me? They were shocked when I showed up with the dead king. Kirill asked me a million questions, then told me to keep my damn mouth shut and fired me on the spot. Not that I blame him. It's my fault he's dead. Irmand gave me a sack of gold and sent me on my way."

Vitali stared deep into the man's eyes but found no dishonesty. He untied the ropes.

Thaed looked up at him. "What do I do now?"

"You'll leave here and be the kind of man Aurel would be proud of. You'll stop drinking. Stop bullying. You'll put that gold to good use."

Thaed nodded. "I-I can do that."

"But first," Vitali continued, "I still need directions."

CHAPTER THIRTY-EIGHT

Thaed moved more swiftly through the city now that he had sobered up a bit. It didn't take them long to make it to their destination—a small, neat-looking house in an otherwise rundown part of town. Most of the homes were faded and looked cheaply built, with thick doors and boarded-up windows, but this house appeared well maintained. Inviting, even.

"Here she is," Thaed said. He stared at the door like it was going to jump out and bite him.

Vitali nodded. "Why don't you wait outside? Like old times."

Thaed sighed in relief. "Thanks. Don't think I could go back in there."

Vitali pushed the door open, and it creaked on bent hinges. There was no lock, Thaed had broken it the day Aurel died, and no one thought it necessary to repair it. The interior was well-maintained, much like the exterior. Small and well furnished. It would have been a lovely place to live, save for the large bloodstain on the ornate rug in the center of the room. Vitali crouched to look at where King Aurel had breathed his last. Nijah was right.

There was a lot of blood.

Vitali wasn't sure what he'd hoped to find here. If there had been incriminating evidence, Kirill would have found it. Or covered it up. Still, seeing this house reminded Vitali what he was up against. This city housed the killer of a king.

He had turned to leave when something caught his attention. A breeze, faint and nearly undetectable, brushed his fur, but it wasn't coming from the open door. It was coming from deeper within the house.

An ornate chair, the kind that looked too expensive and too uncomfortable to sit in rested in the corner. Vitali moved toward it, and the strange breeze grew stronger. He grabbed the arms of the chair and tried to move it aside, but it was bolted to the wall. Strange, for a chair. He pulled hard and the wood began to drag along the floor, bringing the wall with it.

But it wasn't a wall, not really. It was another door.

A small hidden chamber opened in front of Vitali. He stepped inside.

The room was filled with candles burned down to different levels, but Vitali had brought no matches with him. His eyesight was good enough to see in the dark, aided by moonlight creeping in through a small window near the ceiling. The source of the breeze.

If the main room with the bloodstains was nice, this room was extravagant. A beautiful, hand carved bed filled the back wall, a bed too small for an adult. There were heavy-looking toys littering the ground as well, but Vitali's eyes barely registered the nice things. He was too focused on the ugliness.

Burn marks on the silk sheets. Deep claw-like gouges in the wallpaper. A metal horse that looked like it had been crushed by a hand.

What kind of person lived in a place like this?

Before he could think further, he heard Thaed shouting from the main room. Vitali stepped out of the haunted bedchamber and found the man standing before him, out of breath.

"Quick, I need you outside."

Before Vitali could ask a follow up question, Thaed was out of the house. Vitali sprinted after him. He ran through the broken door and into the middle of a ring of people.

There were at least a dozen of them, and they all wore black from head to toe.

"I'm sorry," Thaed told him, his voice breaking. "I had no choice."

"You shouldn't be snooping around here." One of the figures stepped forward. His voice was odd, like he had a recently broken nose.

"Let me guess, you work for Kirill? What's he trying to hide?"

The man in the mask laughed. "Guess you'll never know."

Without a signal, the black masks attacked. Each of them wore metal gauntlets on their hands, and they knew how to throw a punch with them.

Vitali tried not to give them an easy target.

He lashed out with his claws, drawing blood from

someone's stomach. This kept the circle of attackers back, but Vitali knew it wouldn't last.

They came at him again, and Vitali looked like he was going to fight, but at the last second, he bolted in the opposite direction and jumped. A woman reached for him, but he was too fast. He pushed off her head, leaping into the air.

If he could just get past the circle, he could run for it. He was damn fast, after all.

But as he cleared the attackers, a fireball came screaming past him. It clipped his shoulder and sent him spinning to the ground.

He tried to gain his feet, but the black cloaks were on top of him. The metal on their hands and feet pummeled him. He curled into a ball, hoping to lessen the blows.

The last thing he heard before he passed out was Thaed whimpering, "I'm sorry, I'm sorry, I'm sorry."

CHAPTER THIRTY-NINE

Aliz's words were still dancing in Hannah's mind as she climbed the stairs to the great hall. Her words and her face. She just couldn't make out the difference between this young girl fighting for the soul of her city and her not so long ago. But still, something felt not quite right about the entire situation.

Hannah passed a few natives of the city as she marched down a back hallway toward her suite. She turned a corner into a particularly dim corridor, and as she did, a hand grabbed her from an alcove to her left. Another hand clamped down over her mouth.

The fighter instinct kicked in, and Hannah knocked away the hand muffling her cries for help with a quick shift of her forearm toward the ceiling. At the same time, she drew up a thick shaft of ice with a deadly frozen point in her right hand as she pinned her assailant against the back wall.

"Whoa, whoa, whoa," Parker shouted. "It's me. It's me."

"If this is your idea of some sort of romantic rendezvous, you should consider what date night might be like with an ice spear driven through your leg. I was about to pulverize you," she stated as she lowered Parker back to his feet. Then she stepped up and whispered in his ear, "Not that a few minutes of romance would be such a bad thing."

She stepped back, and Parker straightened his shirt. "Sorry about that." He grimaced. "I should know better by now. I'll have to develop a strict training regimen for our kids. Rule one: Don't surprise your mother. Ever."

"Kids?" Hannah asked with a slight smile. "I'll put that on the agenda to talk about on date night. Now, what's up?"

"Something's going down," he whispered. "Follow me." Parker glanced over his shoulder and asked, "Can you give us a little something to quiet our steps?"

"I'm already on it," Hannah said, her eyes burning red.

They moved silently, footsteps muffled by physical magic, down a series of hallways until they stood outside an oak door. It was ajar, and they could hear Irmand and Kirill talking on the other side.

"We've been working the girl all day now, and she still refuses to give up names. That means we know nothing about the other Blue Scarves, what they're up to, or even how many there are. She's tough as nails and as stubborn as a mule."

Hannah heard Kirill snicker. "She can be as tough as she wants as long as you keep her behind those bars for just a little bit longer. It really doesn't matter if we find the others. After tomorrow, they will all know full well not to mess with us. We will show our might and our resolve. The

Mylek people and any others assaulting our city will know who's in charge. You just have to make sure everything is ready."

"Absolutely," Irmand agreed. "We will execute the traitor at dawn."

CHAPTER FORTY

Hannah paced in her room. Parker sat watching her. It had been a long time since he'd seen his girlfriend this concerned, which said a lot since she had saved Irth a few times since they had left Arcadia.

"Shit," she said, finally taking a break from her pacing. "We can't let them execute her. We can't."

"I like it as much as you do, but she broke their laws. What did you expect them to do once they caught the fearsome leader of the Blue Scarves?"

"She's just a kid," Hannah protested. "And what she was trying to do isn't much different than us in Arcadia."

"You never tried to burn down the city," Parker pointed out. "You *protected* innocents."

"*I* had Zeke to guide me. To help me harness my rage and my power. This girl has no one she can trust."

Hannah started to pace again.

"I get that," Parker replied. "But what can we do?"

"I could blow those cells wide open," Hannah suggested.

Parker laughed. "There's that. But then the city will hate

you as well as each other. I thought we were aiming for peace here. Justice?"

"And letting her get killed is Justice? Kirill doesn't care about that. He just wants to look good before the election. For all we know, this execution is nothing more than a distraction. Kirill doesn't want anyone to ask the real questions."

"Like, who had the most to gain from Aurel's death?"

"Exactly." Hannah sighed. "For all we know, Kirill is the murderer."

Parker stood and crossed the room, then took Hannah's hand in his. Mostly, he just wanted to stop her pacing. But he also knew that she needed something now. She needed connection.

"I'm with you. And more than Aliz, I'm worried about what happens to the city if she dies. No way the Blue Scarves back down if their leader is killed. And I don't think Irmand and Kirill give the rest of the Mylek enough credit for their strength and resilience. Kirill is hoping to quash a rebellion, but he could be creating a martyr. It's only one small step from small acts of civil disobedience to civil war."

"This city needs a leader it can trust," Hannah commented. "It's the only thing to stop the fighting. Hell, maybe Kirill *is* the best one for that, but no one can trust anyone until we know who killed the king."

"Any word from Vitali?" he asked.

"He's still looking," Hannah replied. "And I trust that he'll get answers. We just need to give him time. Time we don't have."

Before Parker could respond, the door burst open. A

drunk and laughing Karl and Aysa came stumbling in. Karl dropped his hammer on the hardwood floor and settled onto a couch as Aysa leaned against the wall, bolas still spinning in her hand. Sal bounced in after them.

"You two should've seen this little runt bastard out there tonight," Aysa began, her body shaking with laughter. "He was in rare form. Real rare."

Karl looked at Parker and Hannah and sobered up faster than he could finish a pint of mead. "What's wrong?"

"We need to figure out a way to bust Aliz out of her prison cell," Hannah told them.

"What?" Karl groaned. "Why? Ye just caught her."

"Because it's the right move. And it just might keep the city from blowing itself up."

"Can't we get a moment of rest?"

"Pay no attention to the drunken rearick," Aysa suggested, still giggling. "Let's go bust her out. Right-bloody-now."

Parker's mind was racing. The Bitch and Bastard Brigade had rushed in many times before. They'd always came out on the other side smelling like roses, but this wasn't just one battle, it was the life of the city. He realized that this time, things had to be different. More cautious.

"We can't do that," he warned. "We can't just charge in. Right now, Hannah is the only thing keeping the city together. Both Mylek and Myrna trust her. Some of them freaking worship her. She takes an obvious side, the Myrna lose all trust in her."

"So, what? We let her rot?" Karl asked.

"No," Parker countered. "If she stands by during what

the Mylek see as an unjust execution, Hannah will lose their trust. We just need to move forward with finesse."

Hannah nodded. "We need to free her while making it look like we were completely innocent."

"Okay, so what's the plan?" Aysa asked, leaning over to scratch Sal behind the ear.

Parker smiled. "Better sober up because this is going to be a little tricky. I'm going to need you and Karl at the top of your game." He turned to Sal, who was enjoying the scratches from Aysa's nails. "And *you* are going to need to be *udderly* believable, dragon."

CHAPTER FORTY-ONE

The smell of fresh pine filled Aysa's nose as her eyes drifted over the joints of the newly constructed platform taking up most of the town square. By any measure, the stage was enormous, meant to indicate the significance of the act that would take place on it. Kirill had an eye for flair and knew how to talk to his people.

A hangman, face covered by a thick black veil, stood next to a perfectly tied noose that swung only slightly in the breeze. His hand was on the lever that would activate the trapdoor beneath the victim.

Kirill and the rest of the council were finely dressed for the occasion, eyes cast down the main thoroughfare. The city leaders waited for the procession to commence. However, Kirill's eyes kept scanning the crowd, counting the participants of the show that he thought would solidify his influence.

Aysa knew the man was disappointed. Many had not shown up for the occasion, whether due to a conscious decision or pure disinterest, she couldn't know.

Ky stood next to him, her gaze downcast. One of the Mylek, one of her own, was going to the gallows. Aysa could only imagine what Ky was feeling, and how her gut must be churning. But if the Bitch and Bastard Brigade had anything to say about it, there would be no execution this day. A show? Absolutely.

"I've seen a bigger crowd at a wee rearick's birthday party," Karl said as if he knew precisely what Aysa was thinking. "And them parties were boring as all hell."

Parker nodded. "True. But Kirill is not going to waste the moment."

The deed would be done, and people would talk about this day, possibly forever. He was banking on word spreading. Aysa couldn't help thinking how this was all going to backfire on Kirill in the end.

Aysa felt Hannah's and Sal's absence. She looked up at a small turret overlooking the square. On top of it, she could see a silhouetted figure standing tall, covered in a long cloak, its edges pushed about by the morning wind. Two tiny lights glowed from beneath the person's hood, testifying to the magic within their blood. "I imagine there's going to be some fireworks. At least, if we have anything to say about it."

"Aye, there the lass comes," Karl said, pointing toward the main promenade that led into the square.

The beat of drums and the rhythm of boots marching rang out as the audience turned to see a perfectly executed procession of the Guard coming toward the hangman's platform. It was as if they had practiced for months for a moment such as this. As they neared, the crowd broke ranks, making a pathway for the lines of guards. As the procession turned a corner, Aysa saw what everyone had come to witness: Aliz in chains, sitting on the back of a thick, lumbering steer.

"Pretty sure that's an ox," Aysa whispered.

"Not now," Parker shot back before the rearick could engage with her.

The beast tromped along, taking its time getting to its destination. The condemned girl, not much older than Aysa, sat proudly, was silent, face drawn tightly with resolve. There wasn't a chance she was going to give Kirill or his people the gift of showing even a hint of fear.

While Aysa didn't actually know the girl, she couldn't help but have at least some level of respect for her. Aysa could still feel some lingering pain from burns Aliz's fire had caused her and knew that the flames had meant losses for many in the community. Looking back down at the beast and then taking a glance at Hannah, Aysa said to her friends, "It seems to be working." She squeezed her eyes shut and opened them again, squinting as she looked at the details of the mighty beast. "Maybe a little too well."

"*Scheisse*! Aysa! Shut it, girl. And get ready. It's almost showtime."

"Almost?" Parker shouted with a wink at his friend. "I think it's time right bloody now, you tiny-ass pipsqueak half-breed. If you don't stop looking at her like that, I'm going to take this spear and make you today's first offering to the Matriarch."

The crowd shifted, their gaze turning from Aliz to the man from Arcadia. A low murmur went through them. Aysa grinned, thoroughly looking forward to their theatrics, and more so the fight that would follow. Her hand instinctively on a set of her bolas, she looked up at Kirill. But the son of the king wasn't looking at them. His eyes cut from the steer to the woman on the turret and back.

"Make it quick," she said under her breath to her friends.

"I'd like to see ye try, ye lowlander son of a bitch. Yer hardly a month off yer ma's teat. Ye really think ye can handle this?" Karl's voice boomed louder than Aysa had ever heard it. He sounded like a caricature of himself. But as he drew up his hammer and raised it over his right shoulder, even she felt nervous for the Arcadian.

A circle spread around the two men, like it would at a fight at the schoolyard. The only thing the crowd would want to see more than an execution was two outsiders beating the hell out of each other. Parker stepped back in a defensive stance and raised his spear over his head. The blue tip glowed with the power of Etheric energy.

"Better to be recently whelped than half in the grave, like you are, rearick. You've disrespected the lady and me for far too long. It ends now!"

"Yer mother's not here to wipe yer ass or yer tears." Karl snorted, then sneered. "But I'm happy to smack that look off yer damn face and teach ye a little respect. In fact, it would be me pleasure."

Parker pulled the trigger on his spear and shot a stream of energy over the heads of the congregants. It exploded in a display of blue fire and cracks of thunder. The spectacle drew a collective gasp from the crowd.

Aysa's head spun on a swivel. The crowd had come for blood, and now they hoped they were going to get it at the hands of the foreigners, even if this was just the appetizer before the main course.

She wondered if they had ever made a plan that had gone this smoothly. As the men continued to shout curses and blasphemies at each other, Aysa looked back up at Hannah. Her eyes were still glowing red, and she knew that even for the woman with the Matriarch's blood running through her body, using mental magic on the crowd was taking an extreme amount of energy.

Aysa could only hope there was some to spare in case shit went sideways.

And as usual, it did.

Vitali woke to the sounds of metal chains rattling.

It took him a few seconds to realize that the chains were his own.

He was in a dark cell of some kind. The moist air and cool ground suggested a subterranean cavern. The fact that it was pitch-black made it hard to guess the time, but based on how sore his arms were, Vitali guessed he must have laid here for hours.

Or maybe he was just in pain from having a dozen people jump him in an alley.

He sat up as far as the chains would let him and tried to assess his injuries. Bruises covered his body, but nothing seemed broken.

Although that fact could change. Something about his accommodations told Vitali the black masks didn't bring him here for tea and biscuits.

"I'm sorry. I'm sorry. I'm sorry."

Vitali's cat-like eyes adjusted quickly to the darkness. It

didn't take him long to find the large man rocking back and forth on the floor.

"Thaed," he whispered. No response. "Thaed," he said again.

"I did what I was told," he wailed, but not to Vitali. Thaed was talking to himself. "I did what they said. I gave them the outsider. They have to let me go. They have to. I did what they said."

"Who, Thaed?" Vitali asked. "Who told you to give me up? Where are we? What do they want?"

"I'm sorry. I'm sorry."

Thaed wasn't going to give him any answers, but they weren't alone in this dungeon.

"Isn't it obvious?" a voice called from across the room. Vitali turned and found the old Mylek woman in chains. Vitali smiled despite their situation.

"Nijah. That's twice I didn't see you."

"We might not get a chance at a third time," she remarked with a pained laugh. "They're rounding everyone up. Everyone who knows the truth about Aurel."

"What truth?" Vitali asked, his voice raised. "Who would go to this length just to hide a mistress?"

The old woman opened her mouth, but before she could answer, bootsteps invaded their cell. Vitali could hear them clearly through the thick door.

They entered.

"Well, well, well. Making friends in the dark, are we?"

It was the man who'd led the attack on Vitali. The Lynqi recognized the broken-nosed voice. Two other figures were with him.

"What can I say?" Vitali sneered. "I'm an amiable

person. Why don't you take these chains off, and I'll show you just how amiable I can be?"

The man laughed. "Glad to see my boys didn't knock all the fight out of you. That will make what comes next all the more fun. But you'll have to be patient. We have prior arrangements."

He nodded at Thaed, and the two figures flanked him. They unshackled him from the wall and tried to make him stand, but his legs gave out.

"No. Please, no. I did what you asked."

"What you did," the man shouted, "is tell this outsider about the king. Now we're going to find out who else you told."

"I'm sorry," Thaed cried out. "I'm sorry, I'm sorry, I'm sorry."

The man in black laughed. "Not yet, you aren't. But you will be."

He left, and his lackeys dragged Thaed behind him. Vitali heard his screams echoing down the hall.

"Like I said." Nijah sighed. "Tying up loose ends."

"But Thaed wasn't lying," Vitali said. "He doesn't know anything. Not really."

"He's too stupid to know much," she said. "But he knows enough to cause problems. He knows enough to point you toward the truth."

"The house," Vitali said. "The room."

"What did you see?" she asked.

Vitali told her in detail what he had found. The blood, the scarred walls, the hidden room. She listened intently, then fell silent for a long time. Finally, Nijah spoke.

"There were rumors not quite twenty years ago, before Aurel was king. But I never believed them."

"Rumors of what?"

"A secret love. A woman Aurel was forbidden to be with."

"I don't understand," Vitali said. "He was the heir to the throne. I thought royalty could do whatever they wanted."

"No one in this town is free to do what they want," she told him. "And that goes for the future king. He was forbidden from being with his love because she was like us. A Mylek. The Myrna and the Mylek don't mix, especially not when the royal bloodline is concerned. But like I said, that affair was just a rumor. Aurel married a Myrna woman, became king, and that was that."

"Apparently not," Vitali replied. "He loved that other woman enough to visit her nightly. To lavish gifts upon her."

"I told you," she said. "Aurel was a good king. A good man. He would never betray his wedding vows. Never."

"Then who was he visiting every night?"

Nijah fell silent again. What she said next, she said in a whisper.

"The hidden room. You're sure of what you saw?"

"Yes," Vitali answered. "It was beat to hell."

"Our kind, the Mylek; our powers don't appear until we grow to adulthood. It's a difficult transition. Those markings you described are not uncommon in the bedrooms of Mylek children. Power flows into their bodies, and they need to find an outlet."

"But the king wasn't murdered by a Mylek. There were no wounds, and no offense, but the body magic your people perform is far from clean. He was killed by physical magic, I know it…"

He left his thought hanging as his mind considered his words.

He knew why the coverup was so important.

"He had a child with the Mylek woman."

"Yes," Nijah whispered. "You see now. All kings have dalliances; that's to be expected. Lauded, even. But a scandal like this would be powerful enough to tear down a royal lineage. And what do you think that lineage would do to defend itself? To protect its secrets?"

Before Vitali could respond, the door opened again. The man in the mask returned with his goons and went straight for Vitali.

"It's time we learned what you know, catman," the man said. "I'm going to enjoy this."

CHAPTER FORTY-THREE

Hannah concentrated on the people below. No one screamed at the sight of the giant dragon walking their criminal through the crowd, so her spell was working. She could hear Parker's and Karl's shouts from where she stood. Their half-assed acting would have made her laugh if she didn't have bigger fish to fry.

She paused a beat to glance at Kirill on the stage. Arms waving in a fury, the prince was clearly directing his men from a distance. It wasn't toward Parker's and Karl's ruckus, though, but toward the prisoner. Toward Aliz. She thought it strange for an instant.

Sacrificing a drop of her deep well of intention, Hannah turned her mind toward Kirill's. If there were any moment for her to slip in, this was it.

The city is my responsibility now.

The city is my responsibility now.

The city is my responsibility now.

Kirill's voice echoed on and on in her mind. And as it did, she felt a scratching at the base of her skull, just beneath her ear, as if a small creature were trying to escape.

Something about the way he stared at Aliz felt wrong, and it took Hannah a moment to key in on it. He wasn't focused on the prisoner, he was focused on Sal. He grimaced.

Does he know? Hannah wondered. *Why would my spell work on everyone but him?*

"The hell?" she mused, but her consideration of the oddity was short-lived.

The ground beneath her began to shake.

To make one person believe Sal was an ox carrying a lamb to the slaughter would be like a simple card trick for a con artist in the Boulevard, but to make an entire city believe was a different story. It took extreme concentration, concentration that threatened to slip as Hannah tried to hold onto the shaking building.

Hannah's head shot up, and her glowing red eyes scanned the rooftops below her while still keeping the crowd entranced.

Blue Scarves, dozens of them, stood on rooftops overlooking the city square. Each of them had enlarged hands, enhanced by their power of body manipulation. They banged on the walls of the buildings they had climbed, sending vibrations through the crowd and fear into the hearts of the common folk, who could only guess what these oppressed people had in store.

"Son of a bitch," Hannah whispered. "Aliz had her breakout planned."

Keeping a portion of her energy focused on her ruse, Hannah took two steps and leapt from the turret on which she had positioned herself. Eyes burning brighter red, she called on her magic, and a wind swept up and around her, allowing her body to drift down into the crowd to exactly where she wanted to land.

"This shit is getting real," she shouted to her friends over the rising shouts and cries of the crowd. Men roared, and children wailed. Hell was breaking loose.

"Plan B, then?" Karl asked.

Hannah nodded.

"I didn't think we had a plan B," Aysa spat.

"We didn't," Hannah answered.

"The Blue Scarf!" a voice rang out over the din. "She's fucking gone!"

Hannah looked over and saw the truth. Aliz was no longer on Sal's back. For a second, the crowd was silent.

"Did our plan work?" Aysa asked.

"No," said Parker. "But someone's did. Our prisoner has flown the coop."

"*Scheisse,* lass. This ain't good."

"I hate to say it, Karl, but I think you're right," Hannah said in a hushed voice.

Kirill was screaming bloody murder, sending the city guards to push through the crowd. But given how tightly they were packed in, there was nowhere to go, and the crowd started pushing back.

"For the Mylek and Solyr!" another faceless voice shouted, and then another, and another.

"I say, hang all the Mylek scum," someone shouted back.

The crowd worked itself into a fever pitch, and Hannah could feel the tension pull as tight as an archer's bow. Then the first punch was thrown.

"Shit. Shit. Shit." Parker grabbed her bicep. "Plan C?"

"We had a plan C?" Aysa inquired.

"We do now," Hannah replied. "You guys make sure everything is secure here," Hannah instructed her team. "People are freaked, and there's no telling what kind of shit is going to go down. Keep the innocents safe."

"Which ones are the innocents?" Parker asked.

Hannah shrugged. "Hell if I know. Go with your gut. It's been tested many times."

She turned away from her friends and walked toward Sal.

"What are you going to do?" Parker asked.

"I wanted to keep Aliz safe until we learned the truth, not set her free. One wrong move now, and this city will explode."

Hannah nodded toward the scaffolding, where Kirill was still directing his men. One member of the platform party was clearly missing, and she hadn't seen him since the riot had been quelled.

"I'd bet anything that Irmand is going after Aliz. Can you imagine how the city will react if he brings her back with a new sword-shaped hole in her chest? I've got to get to her first." Hannah stepped up to Sal, who was still walking in clumsy circles like some drunken livestock. "Nice job, boy, but I need my dragon back. Help me find Aliz, and there's some kaffe in it for you on the other end."

Hannah jumped onto his back, then Sal ran in a circle as if he were chasing his tail, took three steps, and leapt into the air. Wings beating, he shot heavenward, and before Hannah knew it, they were soaring high above the buildings. Sal, being no stranger to reconnaissance, started to circle the city. First, he turned in tight revolutions that focused on the center of Solyr, only to expand out farther.

Hannah stared down the city streets, which were still alive with unrest from the commotion caused by the Blue Scarves. She trusted that her team could take care of things here. What she didn't see on the ground was any evidence of Aliz or the other Blue Scarves. The girl had a lead on them of at least five, maybe ten minutes. She easily could've gotten underground in the city during that time, but Hannah had a feeling the Blue Scarves would not meet within the city walls. It was risky. She and her team didn't gather in Arcadia, where their exposure would be unnecessary.

She gave Sal the command, and he banked out over the city walls and began a circle that swept the landscape. Much like when Hannah and her crew had entered the city, the outlying territory was quiet. Still. The threat of pirates and other marauders held people's hearts. There was safety within the city gates. Even for the Mylek, even if their comfort was only relative to being out in the violence beyond the walls.

Sal continued his loop until suddenly bearing hard to his left.

"What is it?" Hannah asked, her eyes scanning the horizon. It took a beat before she realized what her dragon had perceived far faster than her human senses could. Whether it was his keen eyesight or the dragon's heightened sense of smell, Hannah would never know. It didn't matter. He saw it.

Sal was leading her toward a tiny spire of smoke coming up out of a small outcropping of rocks a hundred yards off. She slammed her open palm against the side of his scaly body. "That's my boy," she yelled.

Sal jerked his head up and down, pleased at his ability to solve his friend's problem, and maybe even more happy to know he would be having his drug of choice later that evening.

Hannah laughed. "It's not a done deal yet, pea brain."

As Sal approached the rocks, a tiny path came into view. It wound through the trees and could have been easily confused for a deer trail or the path of a wild boar. Sal hit the ground running, then put on the brakes. Hannah was already on foot by the time he skidded to a stop. With her dragon right behind her, Hannah walked the rocky path to where they saw the smoke rising. Within minutes, the path terminated at the dark, ominous mouth of a small cave.

"Sorry, boy. Looks like the journey ends here for you."

Sal gazed at the narrow entrance, then got down on all fours, scrunching his body like a child pretending to be a pup. He wagged his head up and down, clearly desperate to go with her.

Hannah couldn't help but laugh. "I know, boy. I know you want to. Listen, I'll have a piping hot batch of kaffe for you later tonight, but for right now, I need you to go back. Find Parker. They might just need you there."

The dragon forced his body to constrict even further. He seemed impossibly small, but not small enough to make it into the hole. Hannah gave him one more pat on the side. "Thanks, buddy, but this just ain't happening."

Sal gave her a quick nod, then his forked tongue shot out from between his razor-sharp fangs and smacked her on the cheek. Hannah loved the sign of endearment, even if it almost knocked her over each time

"All right." Hannah chuckled. "Get out of here, now. I'll send a message to Parker if I need you."

Not wanting to argue with the overgrown newt any longer, Hannah stepped toward the cave and crawled in. After a dozen dirty feet on her belly, the passageway opened up. Before she knew it, Hannah was standing.

That's better, she thought. The corridor was a straight shot in.

She produced an orb of blue light with a twist of her hand and set it hovering ahead of her in the cavern. The floor was well-worn, and thankfully, for the first couple hundred yards, there was only one path. But just as Hannah was congratulating herself on how easy the whole thing was going, the path split. She cursed and chose to go the right. She only realized she'd chosen wrongly when the corridor came to a sudden dead end.

"Dammit."

Realizing she had chosen the wrong path, Hannah turned and hurried back down the cave. As she moved, she did a mental scan of the area around her. While she couldn't pick up on specific thoughts, she could sense one sentient creature underground with her. Whoever it was, they were amped up and ready for action.

That must be her, Hannah thought.

She passed the intersection where she had taken the wrong turn and went a few steps down the other path before she felt the tip of a blade against her spine.

"Don't try anything," the gruff voice said. The baritone was laced with confidence.

Hannah raised her hands overhead. "You know I could bring down a fury second only to the Matriarch's right now and tear your body to shreds with a single turn of my hand, don't you, Irmand?"

The cold steel held steady on her back. "Doesn't change a thing. I've got a job to do."

Hannah smiled. "So do I. And you need to know, I don't stand around with my hands up for long."

"I doubt you do. You're not just powerful, you're also smart."

"And pretty," she shot back with a grin. "Most people add pretty."

He ignored her. "I'm banking on the fact that you're smart enough to know you and I have come here for the same reason."

"I came here to stop you from doing something stupid," Hannah told him. "Looks like I already failed."

He laughed. "I will find that girl, and she will be brought to justice. She's a threat to my city."

"Maybe," Hannah said. "But she's not the only one." Hannah put her hands down at her sides.

She considered doing precisely what she had threatened and launching a magical assault on the captain of the guard, but there was just something about Irmand. As bumbling as he had been during the fire in the apartments, Hannah could tell he was driven by good intentions. Pathway to hell or not, good intentions could still demonstrate one's true character. "Lower your blade, Irmand. Let's go find the girl together. And then we will settle things once and for all."

She felt the end of the blade retract from her back, and

she turned to face him. "Now we are getting somewhere." Waving her hand in front of her in the direction of the hole, she told him, "After you."

Irmand was either smart or scared, or maybe a bit of both. He stepped in front of her and led the way down the hall. The captain remained quiet, and Hannah couldn't be sure if he was guarded or terrified.

Finally, he said, "I imagine that when we find her, regardless of her situation, you won't let me take her in. Will you?"

Hannah considered the question for a beat. She pictured the girl standing on Kirill's brand-new execution platform, noose around her neck. Then she thought of Adrien and the years of abuse he had heaped on Hannah and her people.

"I've been in her shoes," Hannah informed him. "That's all. If she's the villain you say she is, I will deal out the punishment myself."

"You saw what she's capable of. What her people are capable of. They're dangerous."

"And how will these dangerous people react when you bring back the dead body of a girl they seem to love?" Hannah asked. "Kirill hasn't thought it through. His execution almost started a riot. If you bring back her bloody body, the city will explode. And they'd be right to. Is this who you signed up to serve? A king who kills without any real process?"

Irmand didn't say a word. He stood silent, and Hannah could only presume that he was considering her message.

"So, you knew about this place, and you knew Aliz would be coming here," Hannah finally said.

Irmand shook his head. "This place? Of course, I didn't. If we'd had any clue about the whereabouts of the Blue Scarves, we might've been able to root them out weeks ago. I saw you and your dragon leave the town square, and figured I'd follow my gut. I'm only here thanks to you."

"Wait, you kept up with a flying dragon?"

Irmand laughed. "We have these natural things in our part of the world; you might have heard of them. They're called horses. Mine happens to be particularly fast."

Hannah smirked. "Properly speaking, Sal is also 'natural.' At least, at root, he is. But enough dithering about our steeds. Are we going to do this or what?"

Irmand nodded. "Follow me." He headed down the hall, and Hannah allowed him to lead again. She thought he could do less harm in front of her.

They arrived at a door built into a spot in the corridor that had been hewn more carefully than the rest of the cavern. Irmand raised his sword with his right hand and reached for the knob with his left.

"By the sword was not our agreement," Hannah reminded him.

"The Blue Scarves are a merciless bunch. You should not expect to cross this threshold and be greeted by drinks and snacks. Once I open this door, all hell might break loose. I prefer to be ready."

Hannah said nothing, and her silence must have told Irmand to proceed. The captain of the Solyrian guard threw open the door and rushed into the room, ready to get the jump on his adversaries, but when they stepped in, they found the room empty. There was no Aliz, no anyone.

A single solitary table sat in the middle of the space.

Smoldering embers in the fire burned on the far side. Hannah crossed the room and looked down at scraps of paper lying face-up on the table. Irmand joined her. He scanned them quickly, pausing only on occasion.

"These are their plans."

Hannah nodded. Irmand was right. She noted the drawing of the building that had burned in the middle of Solyr; places were marked out at certain points on the perimeter. She assumed that was how they had coordinated where different members of the resistance would start the fires. Another page had a diagram of the city, arrows pointing down the promenade toward the square. "The stampede?"

Irmand nodded. There were several more pages, and Irmand took the time to tell Hannah about the lesser threats they had dealt with before Team BBB arrived at their gates. There was something in his voice, something broken. He was a man who knew he had somehow failed his people.

For the first time, Hannah felt true empathy for him. She knew the kind of responsibility he shouldered and what kind of weight it could become.

"But what's next?" Irmand asked.

Hannah walked over to the hearth and knelt on the warm stones. She ran her fingers through light white ash close to the fire. "It looks like the future will remain a mystery. Apparently, Aliz, or whoever was here, knew we were coming, and they didn't want us to know what's next."

"Smart," Irmand said. "But why leave the old plans?"

Hannah shrugged. "Could have been due to haste or carelessness."

"Or maybe they wanted us to find them," he replied.

"Could be," Hannah agreed. "Those who traffic in terror for the sake of a cause always want the credit. It gives them more power if you, and more importantly, if Kirill knows they are well-coordinated and resolute. That's how you win this kind of gambit."

Hannah thought back to her own siege against Adrien, his guard, and the nobles in Arcadia. The Blue Scarves' tactics weren't all that different from her own when she and her team were trying to overthrow the regime in her hometown.

"Right," Hannah said, "so the plans have been burned and they're not here, which can only mean they're preparing for the next attack."

Irmand nodded and paced the room. "Each of them has been bigger than the last. I can only imagine that they are going to reach their climax soon, gods help us. There's only one target that they can have in mind for the next act of terror."

Hannah felt her throat constrict. "Aurel's funeral."

"That's right," he answered. "The inhabitants of this city, both Myrna and Mylek, loved the king. The whole damn town is going to be at this event. If they're smart, and they are, that's the next target." Irmand glanced at the fire and the light white ash. "We might not know what they're going to do, but we have a pretty good idea where they're going to do it."

Hannah studied the man's posture and the features of his face. Clearly, he was a citizen of Solyr and a civil servant. If there was nothing else Hannah had become good at over the last handful of years, it was judging character. And as far as she could tell, this was an upstanding man.

"We both came here to bring Aliz in. What's the next move?" she asked.

"We work together. Stop whatever the hell they're planning."

Hannah saw where he was coming from, but still, she was reticent to go all-in on some sort of partnership with the captain of the guard. Even if Irmand was a man of good intentions, she didn't trust Kirill, but she decided to give him a chance. "Let's go. The funeral is only hours away, and I expect you and I both want to brief our teams."

A smile spread on Irmand's face. "Days ago, I figured you for a no-good outsider."

Hannah shrugged. "I figured you for a no-good asshat, so I guess we're in similar situations."

Hannah led them back out through the tunnels toward the mouth of the cavern. She could feel the freshness of the late morning breeze on her face as she pushed through the squeeze and out under the cobalt-blue sky. She wasn't surprised to feel a sense of ease at being outside the cavern, even if she never considered herself the slightest bit claustrophobic. She was, however, surprised to be staring into the beady black eyes of an oversized newt with wings.

"Sal? What the hell? I told you to go back and help Parker," she said almost sternly.

Sal beat his tail on the ground and jerked his head in the direction of a small path that led off into the woods.

"What is it?" Hannah asked, realizing quite well that her dragon had not yet learned to speak. She made a mental note to work on that.

He slammed his tail on the ground again and walked toward the trail.

"I think he wants us to follow him," Irmand interjected.

"No shit, detective."

"Has anybody ever told you you're a smartass?" he asked.

"I don't think I've ever met anybody who didn't call me a smartass." Hannah looked at Sal, who had preceded them down the path. He paused and looked over his shoulder, waiting for his master to follow.

"We don't have time for this," the captain said.

Hannah shook her head. "Trust me, Irmand. When Sal says something is important, it's important. For the most part, that big hunk of scales only wants to lie around eating, sleeping, and drinking kaffe."

"Kaffe?"

Hannah laughed. "I guess the strange brew of the druids hasn't made it this far east. No big. You need to trust me; he isn't a stupid beast. Let's give Sal a few minutes. If it's nothing, we can head back to the city ASAP, but I imagine it will be something big. Maybe something very big."

Hannah didn't wait for him to answer. She took off down the trail behind her dragon. If Irmand decided to go back to town, that was his lookout. She couldn't blame him; they were newcomers after all. She was surprised and maybe even delighted when she heard him grumbling under his breath behind her. But the grumbling turned to silence when the smell of death and decay struck them. The odor swam around them. It felt smothering.

Irmand grunted through the crook of his arm that he

had raised to his nose to block out the odor. "It's a stench from the depths of hell."

"You might be right. Death and hell are never too far away, even on this side of the Madness."

She pushed on and she found Sal in the middle of the clearing, standing with his claws on the edge of a giant pit. Hannah stepped up to it, Irmand at her side. They both stared silently into what could only be called a mass grave. Bodies, naked and entangled, filled half the hole. She glanced at Irmand, whose mouth had dropped open. His face was pale.

"Those…those are my men," Irmand finally stammered. He shook his head. "Yes. They are. I knew each of them by name."

Hannah dropped her left hand to his shoulder and gave it a squeeze. This was the only comfort she could offer at a time like this to a man she hardly knew.

Irmand continued, "Those are them, the ones that we thought had been abandoning our ranks over the past month. I have to say, I find myself ashamed. Valiant men, each and every one of them, and I assumed they had run for the hills with their tails between their legs."

"There's no need for shame, Irmand."

He coughed to clear his throat, and maybe to shove back his emotions in front of the stranger. "But there is. I dishonored these men's names, and now I have my answer. The Blue Scarves got to them. Stripped my men of their dignity."

Hannah looked again at the bodies that lay nude in the open grave. "Their dignity and their bodies. Why take their clothes?"

Irmand turned away from the pit and spat on the ground. "I will find the person responsible for this and hang her by her toenails from the city wall. When Aliz is still gasping her final breath, I will open her from sternum to pelvis and allow her to watch her entrails fall out before the whole city."

"Okay, I know you're upset, but that's still kinda gross."

Irmand looked Hannah straight in the face. "Aliz deserves nothing but the worst. She has not only worked to disrupt our society, but now she has disgraced my men. You say she deserves due process? Perhaps. But once tried, she will face not only justice but vengeance. It's the only way to atone for my failure."

Hannah tilted her head toward him. She could only imagine the man's indignation. For years, she fought beside the most able warriors Irth had ever known. She knew what loss looked like. She was watching a leader mourn the loss of many.

She felt his pain. And his anger.

"You're not the only one who failed. I gave Aliz the benefit of the doubt once. I won't do it again. But the justice you seek will only be found in the city now."

He nodded. "It will indeed, Hannah. Let us go, and let the sword of the Matriarch go with us."

CHAPTER FORTY-FOUR

They dragged Vitali deeper into the tunnels and shoved him into an empty room. Empty, except for Thaed's corpse crumpled in a corner.

"You shouldn't have done that," Vitali said. "You didn't have to hurt him."

"No," said the man in the mask. "But I wanted to."

He nodded to one of his goons, who slugged Vitali in the stomach. The Lynqi's legs were weak, but two other masked figures held him up under the arms.

"I'll make this simple," the man told him. "I want to know what you know, and you're going to tell me."

"Answer a question for me first." He tried to keep his voice calm, as if this were a discussion over kaffe. "What happened to your nose?"

The man laughed. "I ran into a small nuisance the other night."

Aysa, Vitali thought, a smile on his face. *That's her handiwork.*

"If I had to guess, it looks like that nuisance ran into you."

Another metal-enclosed fist to the stomach.

"You understand why we're doing this, right?" the man asked, less as a question than a threat. "We need to maintain order in this city. The Mylek scum want to tear it apart. We're the only ones keeping it together."

Vitali showed his fangs. He imagined what Aysa would say if she were in this situation. "Screw you, asshats. You can do whatever you want to me, but Hannah will find you. You don't know what it means to see something torn apart, but you will."

The man pulled off his mask, his eyes black and full of rage. Vitali could tell he was choosing from a menu of spells he could use on him.

"If that dumb girl you follow is so powerful, why hasn't she seen through Kirill? Our leader has played her like the fool she is. He knows everything. He reads the hearts of men and crushes them beneath his boots. Perhaps your Hannah is not as strong as you think."

Vitali considered that. He knew Hannah could read minds, but she didn't know about Kirill's cover-up, or the goons he had working for him.

"You see?" the man exclaimed. "You're all alone down here. The Queen Bitch herself couldn't save you." He raised a fist, which burst into flames. He held it close to Vitali's face.

"So, I want to know what you know. And you're going to tell me."

Vitali considered making a threat but broke into laughter instead. "I know everything. Everything. I know about Aurel's affair with a Mylek woman. I know your prince is desperate to cover it up. And more importantly, I know why. I know about the child."

The man stood up, shock written on his face.

"You don't know," Vitali said. "All this, and you don't even know what your boss is asking you to cover up? Some leader."

"Shut up," the man snarled.

"Tell me," Vitali continued, "what do you think this exalted ruler of yours will do when this is done? If he went to these lengths to keep this secret, do you really think he'd leave you alive, now that you know? Maybe you're the one being played for a fool."

"I said, shut up!"

The man's hand burst into flames again and he swung at Vitali's face.

Just like Vitali was hoping he would.

Vitali reached out with his shackled hands and wrapped the chain around the man's arm. He pulled hard to the side, the fire touching the cloak of the man who held him on the right. He used his legs, not nearly as weak as he had feigned, to take down the man on his left. Hours of training had paid off.

He was alone with the leader now.

Vitali pulled the chain harder and heard the satisfying sound of the man's arm breaking.

"This is for Thaed."

He pushed the broken arm, still on fire, into the man's chest and held it there until the flames grew too high.

Vitali left the room smelling of burned flesh and hair.

Despite the dark, winding layout of the cells, he found

his way back to the old woman easily enough. She stared at him wide-eyed.

"You really do serve the Matriarch."

"I try my best," Vitali said. He managed to detach the woman's chains from the wall, but like him, her arms remained shackled together. "We better get out of here. There's no telling how many more of those black masks are down here, and with my arms shackled, I won't be quite as capable of holding them off."

"I think I can help with that," she said. Her eyes blazed yellow, and Vitali watched in awe as her arms doubled in size. The metal around her wrists buckled before shattering completely. She snapped the chains around Vitali's hands like common twine.

"Wow," was all he could muster.

"Still underestimating me?" She smiled.

"Never again," he said. "Now let's go. I have to find Hannah. I think I know who the murderer is!"

CHAPTER FORTY-FIVE

Rows and rows of chairs had been set up in the town square, thousands of them. Hannah could only guess that Kirill had called all hands on deck to prepare for the grand funeral of his father. She and her crew stood at the back of the crowd, filled with an anxious itch ever since Hannah shared what she and Irmand had found in the cavern.

Karl, one hand gripping his hammer, muttered under his breath, "Looks like a good place fer a slaughter to me. Whether from them scarf people or Kirill and his ilk, I can't guess."

"All places being equal, yeah. Someone could create a shit-ton of carnage here. That's why we have to stop it before it begins," Aysa replied.

"Aye, and as soon as ye let me know what 'it' is, I'll squash it under me boot."

Hannah kept her eyes on the platform, where Irmand stood next to Kirill. His face was still pale, his body straight as a pole. Just like Karl, his hand was on his weapon, waiting for the attack he had expected would inevitably descend on their citizens.

"Keep your mouth shut and your eyes open," she said to her team. "Karl is right. The people are exposed here. Irmand has assured me his city guard will help us when the time comes."

"Can you trust him?" Parker asked.

Hannah looked at the soldier. "Honestly, I don't know."

As she spoke, a band dressed in the city's traditional garb began to play a dirge from the platform. The council sat in a row of chairs in the shadow of the giant statue of the Matriarch that towered over them, keeping watch. The congregation followed suit and took their seats. The song went on for minutes. Hannah heard sniffles and blowing noses from those gathered.

Then, without warning, from behind them, a mighty horn blasted over the sound of the band, which continued to play a harmony beneath.

At the sound, the council stood once again, and the crowd did the same. In one swift move, Kirill covered his heart with his right fist and raised his eyes toward the back of the square. Everyone assembled followed suit, and the citizens in their seats turned to face the procession.

Slowly, a pair of yoked oxen plodded into the square.

"Hey, is that who I think it is?" Aysa whispered.

Hannah couldn't help but smile as she hushed the Baseeki girl. "Definitely not, so don't wait for Sal to jump out and save your ass."

"I'm sure the big oaf's around here someplace," she continued, her eyes scanning the sky.

"Aye. He always is." Karl grunted.

Six pairs of guards marched ahead of the oxen cart holding their king. Aurel's body, unnaturally stiff and posed, lay on top of a pile of tinder, prepared for the funeral pyre as was their tradition.

The men wore crisp uniforms, swords hanging by their sides. All of them had their eyes raised toward the image of the Matriarch, who looked down on them with a watchful stone gaze. Their feet maintained a rhythm as they moved down the wide path marked out between the citizens and their rows and rows of chairs.

Nearly three-quarters of the way down the aisle, the lead guards stopped. A quiet din rolled throughout the crowd, their silence broken by what seemed like a disruption of the normal ceremony.

"Aye, the hell is this, lass?" Karl whispered.

"Just wait," Hannah murmured, her hand on her friend's shoulder. But her eyes were already blazing red. She'd been waiting for this. For something.

Heads turned in all directions. The disruptions of the Blue Scarves had made everyone in Solyr tentative about events like this, times when they were all gathered. They were called terrorists for a reason.

"For Solyr," one of the lead guards shouted in a voice that seemed to be amplified by a hundred amphoralds.

As he did, the men pivoted toward the citizens and attacked, each of them assaulting a group of Mylek who had gathered to pay their last respects to the king who might have legitimized them in the community.

"Oh, hell, no!" Hannah shouted as she moved toward the attack.

The crowd milled around in a frenzy. Some rushed

toward the fight, some in the opposite direction. She pushed through the churning people, eyes red, mental energy going out over the sea of bodies in an attempt to still their minds.

But there was no response to her mental magic, not even from those standing closer to her.

You reading me? she sent to Parker, who was several rows of people behind her.

Nothing.

Something was out of whack, and Hannah knew that the magic of the mystics was not working.

Just as she was considering what sort of massive magical distraction she would use to calm the crowd, someone beat her to the punch.

A voice filled with strength and rage boomed at those gathered, "Be still!"

The crowd froze in place as if the sun had gone dark before their eyes. They all turned their bodies toward the statue of the Matriarch and stared up at the woman standing on the stone-cast image's right shoulder. Her arms were stretched out over them like a priest before a sacrifice. A blue scarf was draped around her face hiding her features from the onlookers.

But Hannah knew precisely who it was.

The woman pulled the mask down, and an audible gasp came across the crowd.

"Look and see where we have come to!" Aliz shouted, her voice carrying across the town square at an unnatural volume. She pointed at the guards in the middle of the gathering, the ones fighting with the citizens who had come for the funeral. "Your Guard. These men. They have turned on you today, as the city has come to pay homage to our beautiful king. This is just a sign of things to come. The future is here, and it is now. But really, we all know it isn't much different than our past."

She paused, and there was a murmur in the crowd.

"There is a time for all people to make a decision whether to stand or to rollover. The Mylek have prostrated themselves to the power of the Myrna for far too long. It is not their city. It is *our* city. Everyone's city. King Aurel knew this, and that is precisely why his cold, dead body lies before you on that pile of sticks. Aurel had already made the decision to spread the power out, to add representation from all classes and all people to the council. We have evidence of this since our sister stands as our voice among them."

Aliz pointed at Ky, who was standing on the platform, nodding in affirmation. "But you know what? It could not be this way. The ones around Aurel wanted the power for themselves. The power and the rule. They fear us, fellow Mylek. Fear our voices. Fear our arms. Now that the king is dead, they will do all they can to keep us silent. A seat on the council," she pointed at Ky, "is simply crumbs for dogs. It means nothing. It is time for us to rise up against the Myrna scum and take what is rightfully ours. We will no longer be pleased with the scraps we are fed, but sit at the banquet table."

Hannah looked from Aliz, still standing on the statue, to Kirill. His face was red and filled with rage. She glanced at Ky, whose face had dropped in solemn resignation. Aliz was deconstructing everything she had built.

"I'm here to say that Kirill is not going to take my power

without a fight." She pointed at the guards in the middle of the promenade again. "*They* will not take my power without a fight. Rise up, Mylek people. You are powerful. You are suited to rule. Join me and make this sovereignty ours."

From somewhere in the crowd, a shout rang out, and then another. Hannah could feel the Etheric energy welling up in the bodies of Aliz's people; the power buzzed around her like a swarm of bees. Limbs and appendages and features started to twist and turn and reshape.

The first Mylek strike was on the guards who had turned on the people. Massive fists and feet and elbows attacked the armed men, who dropped to the dirt and covered their bodies in hopes of survival.

And then the rest of the Myrna joined in.

The crowd burst into shouts and screams. Some voices cried out in praise, others in horror.

"*Scheisse!* Here we go," Karl spat, raising his hammer.

Hannah scanned the crowd again. Mayhem had broken out, and there were fights in every direction. She looked up at the woman standing on the statue. A sneer laced with satisfaction covered her face.

"I'm going for Aliz," Hannah shouted to the BBB. "We need to stop this. Protect the crowd. Save the innocents."

Aysa's eyes cut around the town square. "How do we know who's who? Who the hell is innocent in this dumpster fire?"

"It's hard to tell," Parker agreed. "Just don't make any lethal decisions."

Aysa nodded. "Okay. Knock them out, don't kill 'em.

Got it." She ran into the crowd, bolas swinging in a tight revolution overhead.

Hannah glanced at Parker. "Get in there. I've got work to do."

Parker nodded. "Be careful."

He seldom said those words to her. He understood her power, and his three syllables rang in her ears. Parker knew what she had come to realize—Aliz was more powerful than any of them had ever imagined.

As her team entered the fray, Hannah knew exactly where she was going. She had to get to Aliz. As she moved through the crowd, she realized Aysa was right. It was nearly impossible to tell foe from friend. Who was at fault in this mess? Myrna fought Mylek, neighbor against neighbor. She stepped through an opening in the mass of bodies, dead set on making it to the statue, when a guard with two soldiers at his side moved in front of her.

"You need to come with us, ma'am," one of them said. "Kirill sent us to protect you."

The contents of his words were filled with kindness, but the tone was nothing of the sort. She glanced up at the platform, where Kirill was shouting directions to his men. Hannah and her people were wildcards in his mind. She knew that. And if the Myrna were going to come out on top, it might just take removing the cards from the table altogether.

"I'm good," Hannah assured him. "I can help."

The second man shook his head. "Sorry. We're not asking."

Hannah raised an eyebrow. "You guys don't understand, do you? I don't take commands. Not from Kirill. Not from anyone. It's not part of my makeup. Now, get the hell out of my way."

The lead guard raised his club.

"Oh, please." Hannah held back on her power, but only enough to not kill the men.

She didn't have time for this bullshit, and with the blood of the Matriarch racing through her veins, she had more than enough power to kick these guys into the next millennium. With a sudden burst of blue energy, she knocked the lead guard out of the game.

The other two looked at their leader for a beat. It was just enough time. Hannah landed a powerful right fist to one man's temple; her strength increased by the energy inside her, he hit the ground. Spinning, she pulled her trusty rearick blade from its scabbard at her hip and placed its tip on the third man's throat before he could cast his own magic.

But instead of black, his eyes flashed yellow.

"What the hell?"

The Mylek ripped the guard's cloak from his body, which now bristled with thick, angry spines. She moved fast, moving her knife aside. Before she had a chance to respond, the two other men were back on their feet, their bodies changing as they ripped their cloaks off.

"You're not city guard," Hannah said. A vision of dead bodies in a mass grave came back to her. She suddenly realized why Irmand's men had been stripped of their clothes before they were killed.

Anger swelled within her. The three Mylek moved fast, but not fast enough. She concentrated, sending out her thoughts to the BBB as she dodged scaly arms and claws.

Blue Scarves have infiltrated the city guards. Aliz has been planning to start the war here all along.

Hannah blocked a kick as words came back to her. It was Aysa.

You still want us to play it soft with the Blue Scarves?

It didn't take Hannah long to consider. She thought about all the damage Aliz's crew had caused. All the lives lost. And now she had sparked a war which threatened every life in this city. She channeled her energy into fire, pushing it out all around her. Within seconds, the three Blue Scarves were little more than charred bodies.

Take them down, she responded.

CHAPTER FORTY-SIX

Hannah pushed through the crowd, convincing herself not to stop at every fight she encountered along her way toward the statue. Her powers were needed for one mission right now, and she couldn't be slowed en route. Hannah had to get to the source of the problem. That meant getting to Aliz.

She had all but convinced herself of that simple fact when she broke through a row of people and found a heap of cowering children in the dust. As she watched, a giant Mylek swung an angry battleax at a Myrna, who dodged the assault.

"Shit," Hannah shouted as she threw her hands toward the children. A blue dome of energy rose up around them as the ax descended.

It bounced off its surface, narrowly missing the kids.

She grabbed the Myrna and drove her knee into his gut. All the air left him. She followed up with a right fist to the face, dropping him out of the fight. Spinning toward the

Mylek, she asked, "The hell are you thinking?" She glanced at the children. He had a look of shame on his face. Hannah shook her head. "There's no time for that bullshit. Make it right. Take these kids and get them out of here."

Without a word, the man complied with Hannah's command. She pushed on through the crowd, each step taking her closer to the statue of the Matriarch and Aliz. Halfway there, she climbed up onto a pedestal that on a peaceful day served as a piece of architectural art in the center of the city.

Today, it served as Hannah's crow's nest. She looked around the city square at the civil war that had erupted within minutes. She spotted Irmand not far off from where she stood. He was shouting, waving his arms, trying to get his men to quell the violence they were waging against the Mylek. It seemed his commands were in vain. Spinning, she found Ky, the Mylek councilwoman, doing the same. She ran from group to group, pleading with her people to end the fight.

Finally, Hannah's eyes ended up on the platform once again. Kirill stood there like a general separated from his troops, shouting commands from a point of safety. His face was red, brighter than she had seen it before, as he spurred his people on, urging the Myrna to fight harder. To fight for their city. To fight for their people. To fight for the way of life they had always known they would refuse to give up to the Mylek, no matter what.

Hannah turned her eyes toward the graven image and lost her breath when she saw Aliz was nowhere in sight.

"Damn mother bitch douche nugget," Hannah cursed.

"If you think that's bad, wait until you hear about my day." Hannah turned and saw Vitali standing right before her.

CHAPTER FORTY-SEVEN

Hannah and Vitali stood back to back as they fought, trying their best to keep the city from tearing itself apart.

"Where have you been?" she shouted as she landed a heavy fist on the ribcage of a Myrna woman who tried to freeze her.

The Lynqi laughed. "That's a tale too long to tell now. What's more important is what I know."

Hannah dodged a bony arm with razor-sharp spines. "Spill it."

"Good king Aurel had a kid."

"I hate to break it to you, Vitali, but you're kind of behind the curve on that one. The prince is that asshat on the stage."

Vitali shook his head. "Another kid. Twenty years ago, he had an illegitimate child with a Mylek woman. I'm pretty sure that kid ended up murdering him."

"Holy hell," Hannah shouted back as she used her magic

to freeze the feet of some asshole carrying a club to the ground. "Who is it?"

"I don't know, but whoever it is, they can shape their body like a Mylek and use physical magic like the Myrna."

"Gotcha," Hannah shouted. "So, keep a look out for fireballs and weird-shaped feet. How the hell did Aurel keep this a secret?"

Vitali shrugged. "He was the king. Plus, it probably helped that he was a psychic."

"What?"

"That's my guess. No one else around here does mental magic, so no one suspected it."

As he spoke, Hannah felt the itch in the back of her head burn, the same nagging pain she had felt since coming to this gods-damned town.

"There's another psychic," she exclaimed out loud.

Vitali looked at her, surprised, but she responded only by closing her eyes. She pushed outward with her mind, pushed past the anger and the fear erupting from the mob around her. She heard one thought ringing out.

This city is my responsibility now. This city is my responsibility now. This city is my—

Hannah pushed harder on Kirill's mind, and the words changed. *This city is mine now. This city is mine.*

He had been fooling her this whole time. She pushed harder, and gasped as saw his true plan unfold. Her eyes opened.

"What?" Vitali asked, worry on his furry face.

"We've got incoming," Hannah said. "Kirill has some new friends."

She looked upward in time to see kites flying through the sky. "Pirates."

CHAPTER FORTY-EIGHT

"Bloody pirates," Karl shouted to Aysa, who'd been fighting by his side since Hannah had left them. "I thought it couldn't get any worse 'an what we had."

Aysa laughed, watching a half-dozen hang gliders land a few yards away. "Worse? At least I know these guys are a bunch of dicks we're allowed to dispose of."

Karl squinted. "What ye know about disposin' of dicks?"

Aysa laughed. "Far too literal, rearick. Leave my innocence out of this. Let's get to work."

Karl was happy to follow Aysa as they plowed their way through the crowd of Myrna and Mylek who were still fighting with one another. The girl was right, it was a true pain in the ass trying to figure out who was on the right side of justice and who needed to have their lights put out. There was nothing Karl hated more in battle than ambiguity, and this city had served up a heaping portion of that shit.

"You take right flank," Aysa yelled, pointing to her left.

Karl snickered. "Guess we'll need some classes when we

get back on the *Unlawful* fer you, little girl. Left and right are hard, huh?"

"Shut up and fight," she yelled.

Karl was glad to comply. He dropped one pirate before he was able to unhook from his hang glider. The second and third were on him before he had time to congratulate himself.

"You again?" one of the pirates said with a sneer. "I thought we were going to get your boat the first time around."

"Aye, and all ye got was yer ass kicked, after all. I guess ye got a little ass left to kick, is that right?"

The second pirate, this one younger than the first, stepped forward with a short sword raised in Karl's direction. "The only one who's going to kick some asses—"

Karl pulled the dagger from his belt threw it at the pirate, landing it in his jugular. The young pirate clenched his hands around the blade as blood pumped between his fingers.

"Anybody else want to tell me what's going to happen?"

The lead pirate stepped up to Karl and swung his sword in a mighty arc toward the rearick. Karl met him with the shaft of his hammer lifted over his head, hands spread wide. Sparks flew as steel hit steel. The man bore down, pushing his blade toward Karl.

"No need to play nice," Karl said as he kicked with his heavy leather boot up between the man's legs, finding the softness of his groin. The pirate's eyes rolled to the back of his head, and Karl took advantage of the moment. He spun his hammer down and it landed on the side of his enemy's knee, making sure that particular pirate would need a peg leg. With one more swing, he took the man out of the game.

Turning, Karl saw an old friend. The giant pirate, a head taller than the rest of the crowd, lumbered toward the rearick. He dropped a Mylek woman with his hatchets and gave Karl a wide, toothless smile.

"Third time's the charm." He laughed.

"I was hopin' ye'd show up." Karl smirked and raised his hammer. "I hate to leave loose ends."

"I'm gonna tear you limb from limb, little man. And then I'm gonna take all those pieces and feed them to my dogs, who will run throughout the borderlands shitting them out onto lonely, vacant ground."

Karl laughed. "Well, that's somethin'."

"Aye, it is," he spat back.

The man raised his hatchets and charged. Karl answered.

The battle raging around them disappeared. All that remained were two men determined to kill each other, and only one would succeed.

Once again, the pirate leaned on his speed and ferocity, hoping to overwhelm the rearick. But Karl decided to change things up this time. He swung wide with his hammer, keeping distance between the two of them, and then suddenly let go. His hammer went flying, threatening to take the pirate's head off. It nearly succeeded, but a quick duck saved the man. While he was distracted, Karl used the opportunity to grab a shield and sword from the ground.

It wasn't his standard armament, but he knew his way around weapons of any sort.

The pirate charged again, and this time Karl let him. He played defense, moving in a circle as the pirate's hatchets smashed uselessly on the shield. Karl lashed out with his sword whenever there was an opening, and within seconds, the pirate was covered in the blood that was pouring out of a dozen small cuts. He redoubled his efforts and made even less progress.

"Come out from behind that shield and fight me like a man!"

Karl stepped back, his only response a laugh, which fueled the pirate's rage. He charged, and Karl shoved the shield toward him, knocking the unsuspecting pirate on his ass.

It was only then, while on the ground, that the pirate realized where Karl had maneuvered them: to precisely where his hammer had landed.

The pirate scrambled to his feet, but it was too late. Karl dropped the sword and shield, and with one smooth motion, he grabbed the hammer and swung. The pirate managed to raise his hatchets in a feeble act of defense, but the force of the hammer was too great.

Karl heard at least one wrist shatter, along with the splintering of the pirate's tools.

Karl drew out a cloth and wiped his hammer off as the pirate pulled himself to his feet, grabbing a spear off the ground with his good arm.

"I made ye a promise," Karl said, polishing the hammer meticulously. "Do ye remember?"

The pirate sneered. "Go to hell."

"I promised," Karl continued, "that I'd do ye the favor of cleaning me hammer before I rammed it down yer throat."

He gripped the hammer tighter. "Well, it's clean, and I'm about ready to shut ye up forever."

"Do your worst," the pirate cried, his spear held before him.

Karl raised his hammer high, but before he could strike, a spear hurtled past him, skewing the pirate as if he were made of cheese. The large man gaped at the spear sticking out of his chest dumbly before falling to the ground.

Karl stared in awe, then turned around to see Aysa smiling at him.

"Too slow, old man."

"*Fuck*, ye blasted Baseeki! I've been waiting for that kill since we got here! Since before we got here! That kill was all I been lookin' forward to."

Aysa smiled wider. "I was worried you'd throw your back out. I was always taught to help my elders. You know, old ladies across busy streets. Kitty cats from trees. Elderly, incontinent mountain men from the hands of dangerous foes."

Karl shook with anger. "If it wasn't fer them bloody innocents to save, I'd teach ye some damned respect, ye smart-mouthed lil' brat."

Aysa laughed, then ran back into the melee. "Then finish your job already. This thing's not over yet."

CHAPTER FORTY-NINE

The melee raged on around Hannah. She stood, eyes darting in every direction. Mylek fought Myrna, and the pirates battled both of them. It was impossible to know who would come out on top, if anyone. In all her years battling injustice, there had always been two groups—the bad guys and her team. But now, she stood in the middle of a mass of innocents fighting each other, their rage inflamed by the rhetoric of Aliz and the idealism of Kirill.

Once she broke through Kirill's mental facade, she saw the truth of his plan to work with the pirates. Even if Aliz hadn't pulled her trick, war would have broken out today. Kirill would have used the attacking pirates as all the proof he needed to secure the power he craved. He would have stood strong in front of a united Solyr. But Aliz had stuck first, and now the pirates were descending upon a city torn apart from within.

And they were happy to join in the fun.

A broadsword arced in front of her, and she parried it with her knife. A blast of ice from her left hand froze the pirate dead in his tracks. She ran and leapt onto a merchant's cart above the battling hordes.

Looking over the crowd, she focused her mental attention, just like Hadley had taught her years ago. To all the people in the gathering, she sent a message. *Myrna. Mylek. You must stop killing your fellow citizens. This is what they want! Work together. Defend your neighbors! Death is at your door.*

Even as she intended the words, she could feel them bouncing back at her. There were still no results from her mental magic. No transmission.

She turned to Kirill, but the mental wall wasn't coming from him. He was too busy screaming orders.

Fuck, she thought. *Who could it be?*

Her head throbbed, the source of the headache right behind her ear. Hannah could tell someone in the immediate vicinity was blocking her. Blocking her thoughts. Vitali had told her Aurel was a powerful mystic. If Kirill had inherited the gift, maybe his illegitimate child had as well.

Her eyes scanned the crowd, looking for her mental assailant. As far as she could see, there was none.

Until her eyes landed on the top of a turret looming over the gathering.

Aliz.

Her arms raised over the multitude. Hannah tried sending another message to all the citizens, but it failed. Aliz smiled wider.

"Holy shit," Hannah spat. She realized the young leader of the Blue Scarves was the source of the blockade. It was the only answer.

Aliz was Aurel's daughter.

Hannah jumped off the cart and fought her way through the crowd. She shoved a blue bolt of energy at the wooden door at the base of the turret since she was unwilling to take the time to check the knob. Its wood burst into flame as though it were dry tinder. She charged through, taking the stairs two at a time.

Her heart beat like a drum as she made her way to the top of the turret. As she crested the last step, she paused at the door leading out toward the young girl she felt incredibly connected to. The girl who seemed to be another version of herself back in Arcadia, fighting for the good of her people. The girl who had sparked this riot. Finally, Hannah grabbed the knob, turned it, and pushed her way through.

Hannah expected to see a sole figure overlooking the square filled with Mylek, Myrna, and pirates, all engaged in bloody warfare. She was surprised to find another person on top of the turret engaged in a fight with the young woman.

Irmand had beaten Hannah to their foe, and now he fought Aliz with an energy she had hardly expected the man to have. He delivered blow after blow with his club, but Aliz parried with a set of long daggers. Her yellow eyes flashed as she moved with the speed and grace of the gymnasts Hannah remembered watching in the Noble District in Arcadia.

It was as if every move had been coordinated between the two of them. Just as she expected the dance to go on into eternity, Irmand pivoted and spun down with an attack toward Aliz's leg.

Hannah held her breath. Time slowed. She knew Irmand's attack had swung in beneath the defensive blades of the leader of the Blue Scarves. But before his steel had a chance to get a taste of flesh, Aliz's eyes turned black, and Irmand's club melted into thin air.

Irmand stood dumbstruck.

"Always underestimating me," Aliz taunted.

She took the opportunity to counter with a blast of brilliant white energy from the tips of her fingers. Hannah's heart leapt as the captain of the guard's massive body hurtled across the rooftop. The woman had the powers of Myrna, Mylek, and mystic.

"Hey, megadouche," Hannah shouted. Aliz turned toward her. "Why don't you pick on someone your own size?"

A sneer spread across the Mylek's lips and her eyes turned as black as onyx. "With pleasure."

"The pleasure is all mine," Hannah assured her.

Summoning the Etheric energy of the nanocytes inside of her, she walked toward her foe. The girl was strong, and Hannah knew not to take that for granted. She twisted a hand in front of her and brought a glimmering ball of energy into her palm. Keeping it small, she focused a mass of power into the little package. Something to finish the fight.

Hannah launched it at her and watched the girl spin to her side. Shards of stones bit at the air as the ball of energy made contact with the knee wall of the rooftop.

"A little slow, but not bad," Aliz remarked. "Nice to fight somebody worth respecting."

Shooting to her feet, she shoved her hands in front of

her. Hannah watched the girl's lips move as a sparkling red orb appeared and churned between her fingers.

"I save this for special occasions." She held the bulb in her left hand and pushed the top of it with her right. Instead of shooting like a projectile, the ball expanded toward Hannah, slowly becoming an elongated form, like the tentacle of some deformed sea monster.

"Really?" Hannah laughed.

The red appendage picked up speed as it approached. With a flick of her wrist, Hannah raised an Etheric shield to ward off the attack.

On contact, the red line didn't even seem to strike the shield, but moved right through, as if it wasn't even there.

Hannah's eyes widened as the red cord struck her in the gut. Warmth spread through her stomach and radiated through all her limbs. Her throat constricted, and she could feel her heart revolt against her will, crawling to a stop.

"What have you…"

Aliz walked slowly toward Hannah as the Master Magician from Arcadia dropped to the stone floor. Aliz knelt next to Hannah. Even with the pain tearing through her body, she could feel the Aliz's warm breath on her neck.

"There are things you haven't seen. Many things. My father once told me hubris paves the road to destruction. I think, for you, this is the truest of truths."

Hannah fought to control her body. Not since she was a child had she felt so out of control. She could feel a warm, dark line of blood leaking out of her nose, down toward her mouth, but she could do nothing about it.

"You see," Aliz continued, "it's only appropriate to use

my special gift on you, the servant of the Matriarch. It's the same spell I used on my father. It ravaged him from within. Caused him to bleed out with no wounds. It is clever, isn't it?"

Aliz laughed as her eyes turned back to their pale blue. Hannah stopped fighting the power tearing her apart on the inside; her body lay limp.

"He was a man of the people, or that was what they said. He cared for the powerless. The poor. But all the while, he locked me away from the world. Hid me from their view. I was his shame, a bastard child born of lust and power. A tryst between the great Myrna Lord and a simple Mylek girl could not be tolerated."

Hannah could feel a battle going on inside her. Everything she had fought for survival. For existence.

"He came to visit, lavishing me with gifts. Sure, I would smile. Thank him. Honor him. But it was all a game designed for his demise. They all loved him. Loved what they thought he was. But the son of a bitch was an actor on Solyr's stage, and my power dropped the curtain and turned out the lights. He got everything he deserved."

"Like hell, he did." Irmand's impassioned voice cut through the night sky. He stood over Aliz, his cloak charred from the energy of her magical assault. "Your betrayal will meet the due process of my blade. Tonight, you will see your father face to face before your descent into hell!"

He clenched his teeth and raised a sword.

She gave a wicked laugh. "Irmand, your loyalty to the old man blinds you. Aurel cared only for the one thing I've never had—*power*. But power shifts. Now it is time for me to take that which is rightfully mine. Aurel is gone. Kirill is a damned fool. This city is in my hands."

"Prove it," Irmand spat, stepping toward her.

Aliz met him with arcing swings of her daggers. He knocked her advance away with the experience of years in military service and then launched his own attack. But she was ready for it. The young woman stepped aside and knocked the captain off-balance.

Hannah watched them engage in martial combat. Aliz was playing with him like a cat with a mouse. She could destroy the man with less energy than a sneeze, but this fight was for nothing but pleasure. Hannah realized that she had met, for the first time in a long time, a formidable foe. Aliz had the strength and ingenuity of the matter-shifting Mylek, able to craft her body into earth-wrecking forms. She had the physical magic of the Arcadians and the psychic magic of the mystics, and then there was the mysterious strength that was currently shredding Hannah's body beneath the skin.

But there was one thing she didn't have.

The gift overlooked by many, lauded by few.

The gift of the druids.

CHAPTER FIFTY

Hannah concentrated on her own corporeal being. Focused on her body. Her eyes grew faintly red, but the redness grew, hotter and stronger. She focused her will, all the energy she'd had from birth, matched and accelerated by the power of the Matriarch. And as she focused, the energy did its job.

It began a rapid accelerated healing process.

She could feel the internal bleeding stop and life coming back to her limbs as she purged Aliz's magic.

Hannah looked up and saw Aliz moving in to finish the fight.

Her eyes blazed black. She directed her hands toward Irmand's feet and cast an enormous surge of blue energy toward the ancient rocks beneath them. The floor of the turret crumbled beneath the Etheric energy.

Irmand disappeared in the blink of an eye.

The girl smoothed her cloak, grinning with a quiet sense of satisfaction.

"The enemy is vanquished?" Hannah asked as she stood, Etheric energy buzzing through her body.

Aliz's head snapped toward Hannah. Her face was twisted with shock and rage, eyes narrowed. "Impossible."

"I thought we were so alike, both of us weapons forged by the injustice of our homes. But you have learned only to kill and manipulate and destroy, which is why you'll never lead this city. A true leader knows how to heal."

Aliz stared at Hannah. "You'll find it hard to heal when I've ripped your head off. This is my destiny, and you're just some foreign bitch."

"Damn straight, I am." Hannah grinned. "I've said words like those before. You know where this road leads?"

"I not only walk this road, but I laid the bricks on which I trod. Kirill needs to meet his end, and no one is going to stand in the way of my people taking back the city. It's rightfully ours. Rightfully mine. Don't you dare try to deny our destiny."

Hannah remained on high alert, but she cocked her head to the side. "Your birthright? This world owes you nothing. Your gift is strong, stronger than I imagined. It's you who owe something to the world, but you'd rather waste it with your petty political intrigue."

"Enough talk!" the girl shouted as she crouched.

She tilted her head back and let out a guttural yell that sounded more animal than human. As she did, her forehead expanded before Hannah's eyes, and two massive horns, like those of the steers on the streets of Solyr, expanded from her skull into deadly points.

"Impressive," Hannah said, moving into a defensive position. "I bet you get all the guys."

Aliz launched toward her.

Hannah gasped at the speed of her first step.

"Shit," she shouted as she launched her hands out in front of her, casting a giant wall of ice between her and the she-steer.

But the twelve inches of frozen barricade did little. On contact, the wall burst into tiny frozen bits of shrapnel.

Aliz didn't slow.

Just before they connected, Hannah jumped, shooting a stream of Etheric energy toward the stone rooftop below her. The blast gave her just enough extra lift to clear the charging horns.

Hannah landed and got on one knee as Aliz stopped and spun toward her.

"*O-fucking-le*," Hannah murmured as she got to her feet.

"Last chance," Aliz growled. Her voice had dropped an octave. "Flee now and leave me to my business."

Hannah couldn't help but laugh. "You have no idea how this works. The Bitch and Bastard Brigade never runs, and Justice is *our* business. Now, be a good little calf and call it a night. Turn yourself in, Aliz. Throw yourself on the mercy of the council. They might go easy on you."

Aliz stood up straight. As her shoulders rolled back, her horns shrank and her head returned to normal. "Before the sun rises, the council will be no more."

She raised a hand, and a massive ice spear grew in her palm. Aliz used her Mylek magic to elongate her arm until it was longer than Aysa's. Drawing it back, she launched the ice spear at Hannah with inhuman strength.

"Oh, hell, no!" Hannah screamed, blasting the javelin from the air. "Ice spear is *my* move."

Aliz drew her hands apart, and a fireball appeared in each palm. She volleyed them at Hannah, who swiped them away as if they were gnats.

Hannah walked slowly and purposefully toward Aliz, and the girl's eyes grew as wide as the harvest moon. Hannah knew she was starting to understand exactly what, exactly who, she was up against.

The girl spun her hands in front of her chest, as she churned a massive swirling stew of energy in front of her. The cloud grew. Hannah could feel the pulsing between them.

"This isn't going to end well for you," Hannah told her. The girl's face twitched, and a flash of emotion swept over her brow.

"That was what Aurel said just before I killed him." She let out an ungodly sound—a cry mixed with laughter and pain. "The bastard thought I loved him. Can you imagine? After a lifetime of being locked away? Of receiving gifts, but having no chance to live outside that room? That prison? Once my powers manifested, I knew it was only a matter of time before he would meet his end at my hand. His death brought me nothing but pleasure. Now yours will be the same."

She screamed and shoved the mass of glowing blue energy at Hannah.

With the power of the Matriarch in her veins, Hannah could have blocked the energy. She could have sent it back at the young woman as quickly as it had come. But she did neither.

Instead, she spread her arms to the sides and tilted her head toward the heavens. A smile twisted her lips as the force of the energy struck her square in the chest. Glowing blue splashed all around her, engulfing her.

She took one step back, receiving all the fury the Blue Scarf could muster.

Hannah tilted her head back down and gazed at Aliz.

Her eyes glowed a deeper, darker red than they ever had before.

"You should have yielded," she said as she shoved her hands at the girl.

The power of Aliz's attack multiplied by the power of the heavens traveled the distance between the women in the blink of an eye. It was just enough time for Hannah to see the look on the girl's face.

Aliz realized she had made a terrible mistake.

And then she was gone.

CHAPTER FIFTY-ONE

Pirates. Magic. People with power pulsing through their limbs.

Chaos surrounded them, threatening to tear the city apart.

Parker could see it all, see the forces of evil at work, but he knew the anger in this city wouldn't win. Not if Team BBB had anything to say about it.

Sal swooped overhead, chasing down the flyers. Parker could hear Aysa's laughter over the noise and figured Karl was nearby cursing each and every one of the pirates to some version of remnant hell. Parker turned to see Vitali fighting back to back with a truly terrifying-looking Mylek woman.

Hannah was nowhere to be seen, which meant she must be kicking ass somewhere. But even with all their efforts, the anger still grew around them. They just needed to uproot its source.

And Parker could see that source, at least in part.

Kirill stood on the stage screaming bloody murder, encouraging his people to turn against their neighbors, fanning the flames of hatred.

Parker figured punching that asshole's lights out would be a good first step on the road to Justice.

He ducked a spear as he pushed through the crowd, sidestepping the violence around him. He had always been good at navigating in tight places.

The stage rested high off the ground, but Parker scaled the wooden frame like it was built for him. A small group of guards held the high ground, bashing the skulls of anyone trying to make it to the top. Parker found a gap near the back and slipped up.

What he saw when his feet got purchase on the oak boards made his knees shake.

Ky was on the ground. Kirill stood over her. Parker had seen her trying to stop the fighting, but stopping the fighting wasn't on Kirill's mind. His foot was planted on the woman's chest. Her body twitched.

"What the hell are you doing?" Parker shouted.

Kirill glanced at him. "I'm taking what's mine." His eyes flashed black, and Parker saw the power flowing from his fingers. Ky screamed in pain.

Parker turned his spear toward him, but the guards attacked before he could get off the shot.

So much for his celebrity status.

Four men with clubs turned on him. Parker barely felt their blows. All he cared about was getting to Ky. Protect the people, that was what Hannah had told them to do. And by the gods, he was going to do it.

He swung his spear wide, knocking one of the guards off the stage and into the murderous mob below. He ducked a club, then fired, blasting two of the guards at close range. They wouldn't get up for a long time, if at all.

The last guard was just a kid. Parker aimed his spear at the young man's face and ordered, "Stand down."

The kid's club shook in his hand, but he wouldn't let go.

"The prince…" he squeaked.

"Screw the prince," Parker shouted. "Your job is to protect this city. Look around you."

The kid did. He saw the angry faces below him as if for the first time, and he turned when he heard Ky scream. Parker took his chance and raced past him.

But he was too slow. Kirill pulled Ky's body up in front of him like a shield, his hands burning with fire. "This city is mine. It's my right, and I'm not going to let you or this Mylek piece of shit take it from me."

He raised his hand to kill the Mylek councilwoman. A scream filled Parker's ears, but it didn't come from Ky. It came from Kirill.

The two members of the council fell to the ground, Ky exhausted from pain of torture, Kirill with a knife in his back.

Standing behind them was Irmand, covered in dirt, debris tangled in his beard.

Parker ran over, but Irmand was faster. The captain checked to make sure Kirill was dead, then pulled Ky to her feet.

"Are you okay?"

"You killed your prince," she exclaimed.

Irmand smiled. "My allegiance is to Solyr and to her future."

They turned to look at Parker, who must have looked more than a little surprised.

"What do we do now?" he asked.

Ky shrugged. "We stop this fight."

CHAPTER FIFTY-TWO

Hannah walked to the edge of the turret and looked down at the chaos beneath. From her vantage point, it was impossible to make out who was who among the melee of Myrna, Mylek, and the asshole pirates, but it made no difference. She knew that with Aliz out of the game, she could twist fate and screw with destiny.

With a turn of her hand, she sent a massive bolt of lightning over the combat below. A shuddering crash of thunder followed. All eyes turned toward her, to see her blazing red eyes and hair whipping in the wind.

Focusing, she sent a message to all in the square. Her head was clear. There was no block from Aliz or murmured words from Kirill.

People of Solyr, hear me now. You need to know the truth. The citizens of your good city have been pitted against each other. Neighbor against neighbor. But this is not the way forward into the light. Your path only leads to a darkness that, left to its own power, might spiral into a chaos worse than the Madness.

A murmur grew below her.

But it isn't too late to change your course. One of your people tried to create a revolution for the sake of her own power. But I tell you now, you do not need to cast off all that you are. Instead, you need to become all you were meant to be. You are strong. You are mighty.

A voice shouted from the ground, praising Hannah's words.

It is time to come together as Solyrians. To restore your former glory, and then march into a future of possibilities that none of us yet know. With united hearts, you can defeat those who would pillage and steal all that you are.

Hannah pointed at a group of pirates who were standing with their knives out. *Take them. Take them now, and tell the world that Solyr will not be so easily destroyed. Tell them that you are one people. One voice. One heart!*

A cry rang out from the town square. Moments later, the sound of steel on steel filled the night sky.

The people of Solyr fought as one.

CHAPTER FIFTY-THREE

"Um, you're going to have to run that by me again."

Vitali glanced at Aysa, confusion plain on her face. He turned to see the same confusion on most of the faces staring at him. The throne room was full. Members of the council, along with prominent Myrna and Mylek citizens, surrounded the BBB. They all stared at him, seeking answers to the confusion that threatened to swallow their city.

Vitali cleared his throat and began again.

"You all know of Aurel's virtues, and now you're beginning to learn of his vices. But his character was formed through and through by his power—his secret power. His ability to read and possibly shape minds."

A murmur filled the room, and whispers turned to groans. Clearly, the citizens of Solyr were less than pleased with Vitali's revelation.

"I find this hard to accept," Ky stated from her seat on the throne. "I have never seen a power quite like that."

She had recovered from whatever wounds she had received during the fight and sat tall, with as much composure as a queen who belonged where she was. Vitali assumed that was fitting. She had won the election by a landslide.

"Well, maybe if ye left yer walls every once in a while," Karl grumbled.

"It's not common," Vitali said, trying for a bit more tact. "But—"

A gasp interrupted his explanation. He followed the council's wide eyes to Karl, who had turned purple. Then green. Then yellow.

"What the bloody hell?" the rearick shouted.

Aysa burst out into laughter as Hannah rose to her feet, her eyes blazing red.

"It's real," Hannah said. "I can make you see things far stranger than a purple rearick. It's a gift of mine, and it's a gift Aurel's kids seemed to inherit. They used it to block my attempts to root out the truth about how the king died."

"Aliz murdered him," Vitali confirmed. "She blamed him for her cursed life, trapped away from the world. She blamed him for his lies, and she hated that the city worshipped him. In the end, she decided to exploit that love to shake up the city."

"But why did our city guard not know?" a Mylek man asked. "How could this have been kept from the council?"

Vitali turned to look at Irmand, who was looking at the floor.

Hannah stepped in. "That was her half-brother's doing. Kirill wanted his father's throne, but he couldn't tarnish

Aurel's memory in the process. He covered everything up, choosing instead to exploit the situation for his own benefit."

Aysa scoffed. "Some kids."

"A monstrous hybrid." An older Myrna man sighed.

"Not a monster, at least not at first," Vitali responded. "Aliz was part Myrna, part Mylek, and without a doubt, her father's daughter. It's no surprise she could rally disaffected Mylek around her. It's no surprise she could plan an insurrection with little political power. In fact, she and her brother seemed to follow the same playbook. Aliz disguised her Blue Scarves as guards to convince reticent Mylek to fight. Kirill had brokered a secret alliance with the pirates to inspire the Myrna. They both sought to sow division. Inspire chaos. Take power."

"She was evil," a Myrna woman said.

"And Kirill was a tyrant," a Mylek man responded.

"Yes," Hannah said, her tone a clear command to shut up. "Kirill was corrupt and Aliz was cruel, but their plans were only possible because of the hatred in this city. A hatred echoed and amplified by the people in this room. There were villains here, but they found a willing city. Every single one of you needs to ask yourselves why that is and what you are prepared to do about it."

Ky spoke once again, breaking the silence. "You are right. Aurel might have been a kind man, but calls for unity without a corresponding course of action will solve nothing. I have earned the votes of this city, but I hold no illusion that I have earned this city's trust. That will take time, but the work starts now." She rose to her feet. "Irmand, step forward."

Irmand rose from the back of the room. He moved slowly, whatever damage he took during the fight seemed to stick with him, despite Hannah's healing. His composure was unwavering, but the whispers filling the room hinted at only one question.

What punishment would the new queen mete out?

"Irmand, you have served this city as the captain of the guard for many years. You have perpetrated harm on your fellow citizens. You followed a corrupt leader's commands. I would ask that you follow mine."

He looked up, his composure shattered. "You're giving me my job back?"

She smiled. "I can think of no one better to help me heal this city."

He grunted and stood a little straighter. "I *won't* fail you."

"I know you won't because I will be watching you like a hawk. I do have one command, however."

"Anything, my queen," Irmand said with a bow.

"You will begin to hire Mylek as well as Myrna for the Guard."

Irmand opened his mouth in shock before closing it again. "That...can be arranged."

Vitali felt the tension in the room ease. *Maybe they can pull this off*, he thought.

Ky looked at Team BBB. "I and all of Solyr will be forever in your debt. How can we thank you?"

Sal's head perked up. He sensed the chance of a treat.

"We need nothing," Hannah responded. The dragon's head dropped. "Except for you to rule well. When I come back here, I expect to see Solyr thriving and not a smoldering heap of ashes."

"Deal," Ky replied. "So, you are leaving, then? Where will you go?"

Hannah looked at her team. "Wherever we're needed."

CHAPTER FIFTY-FOUR

Hannah kicked her feet up on the worn wooden rail as the sun set off the starboard side of the *Unlawful*. Solyr was only a few hours behind them, but she expected that Aysa would keep the ship pushing forward through the night. The Baseeki girl loved the craft, and Hannah knew she had missed wayfinding in the captain's chair.

"Aye, two ice-cold brews, lass," Karl said, as his weight steadied with the shift of the ship. "That freak is at it again!"

Hannah laughed as she grabbed the mug from Karl, watching her friend land in the chair next to her with a huff.

"Would've gotten them arseholes a drink, but who knows how long them wankbags will be at each other." Karl watched Parker and Vitali spar on the bow.

Hannah grinned. "Some things go back to normal pretty easily, don't they?" She shifted a leg off the rail to give her snoring dragon a little kick in the ribs. "Especially this guy."

"That's right, lass. Like any other humans out there, we fall right back into our ways." Karl's eyes stared beyond Parker and Vitali over the bowsprit. "Where we goin' now? Ye even know?"

Ky's last question in the throne room rang in her ears, as did her answer. "Wherever we're needed."

"Bullshite, ye damn magician. We both know better than anybody that we're needed damned near everywhere. We find injustice under the seat of every outhouse we stumble into. But this boat is goin' someplace, and I kinda, for once in me lifetime, want to know where."

Hannah glanced over her shoulder, hoping to catch one last view of Solyr, but it was gone. Like all the other cities they had wandered into and out of, it would be a memory. Vivid, but soon to fade.

Karl landed a meaty hand on her forearm, and a wave of warmth ran through her. The rearick was more of a father to her than her own, who had abused her until the day he met his untimely death. No one, maybe not even Parker, could cut her to the quick as efficiently as Karl.

"Where we goin', lass?" His eyes were filled with compassion, his care not for himself, but for her. And while Hannah thought it might have been the effects of the wind and the setting sun, she swore his eyes were glassing over with tears.

She gave him a slight nod. "Yeah. You're right. I'm wayfinding myself."

"Good. I thought as much."

"We've been on the move for a shit-ton of years, Karl. We have brought Justice to every end of Irth. We've defeated every kind of enemy, and closed doors on world-ending realms. It's time we find a place." She smiled and waited for his response, but there was none. "It is time for us to do what Zeke tried to do so many years ago. It's time to build a home."

Available now at Amazon and through Kindle Unlimited

The gods are real...and they want their world back.

Thousands of years ago, ancient deities fought a civil war that nearly destroyed the earth. They were defeated by a great warrior—and banished to spend eternity beyond the reach of the humans who once served them.

Their war is raging once again.

And once again, it will require a great hero to save humanity.

Unfortunately for humanity, I'm that hero.

My name is Vic Stratton. I'm no saint, but I'm the best chance we've got at surviving the chaos about to be unleashed. But hey, at least I have my good looks, a quick tongue, and the sword of the gods on my side.

And I'm going to need it. Because when the gods return, all hell will break loose.

Read now and discover *The Forgotten Gods*

The Forgotten Gods **Boxed Set includes the entire eight book series:** Forgotten Gods, Goddess Scorned, Hounded By The Gods, God In The Darkness, Gods Of New York, God Country, Haunted By The Gods, and Gods Remembered.

Grab your copy now at Amazon and through Kindle Unlimited

AUTHOR NOTES - CM RAYMOND & LE BARBANT

DECEMBER 15, 2019

Welcome back, friends!

Exactly three years ago to the month, Lee and I hosted THE Michael Anderle on our (now defunct) *Part-Time Writers Podcast*. It was a show in which we were trying to see if we could go full time as authors in 52 weeks.

We were clever and charming (and sometimes half in the bag). At least that's the way I remember it through the haze of time and bourbon.

At that time, we had released our Steel City Heroes trilogy and the Jack Carson series was underway. Man, we were working really, really hard.

During that first year of our very serious production is when the renegade creator of the Kurtherian Gambit Universe, THE Michael Anderle, had totally blown up. Being the all-around compassionate badass that he was, he agreed to come on the show so we could interview him about how in the world his little indie story blew up into a phenomenon… and how we might be able to do the same!

Well, to keep the long story not so short, Michael told

us all the things he thought we did wrong, and everything — from major themes to tiny details — that he thought his fans had fallen in love with in the tales of Bethany Anne. Sure… we wanted to defend Lee's five page description of the steel union strikes in our Superhero book. Who wouldn't?

Through some twists and turns, we went to Michael with our hats in our hands asking if there was a place for a couple of guys like us in the TKG, and the Rise of Magic series was born. Little did we know it would turn into the Age of Magic with a slew of authors and more books than I know at this point.

Over that year, we wrote eight Rise of Magic books and built, brick-by-brick, author-by-author, bird-by-bird the Age of Magic… and had a hell of a time doing it.

After book 8 — *Reborn* — we had all but assumed that the series had ended.

Sure, Hannah and friends would show up in someone's series from time to time to kick some ass. But they'd done their jobs, and we had other books to write.

But we should have known, Hannah would not be retired!! Two years later and here we are…

Now, where to?

Honestly, I have no idea. Not yet at least.

What we do know is that *Solyrian Conspiracy* ends with a bit of a longing. With Hannah and Parker's desire for a place of their own. A place to settle down. I'm already kicking around how the hell this can happen… and maybe, better yet, where. Maybe by the time you read this, the book will be ready for purchase. But for all of our early readers, this one is going in the creativity crockpot for a couple of months on simmer.

Meanwhile, Lee and I will be releasing two more books in the Steel City Heroes (which has been torn apart and rebuilt from the ground level) and a new urban fantasy thriller series, which is just about to get underway!

So... thanks to our JIT readers, editors, and amazing cover designer, Miha. Thanks so, so, so much to Michael Anderle for taking a shot on us years ago. But, really, the major portion of our gratitude goes to you, our readers. None of this happens without you.

We are forever grateful!

For Irth,
Chris and Lee

PS: As usual... we ALWAYS love reviews. So, you know the deal. Imagine Lee grovelling.

PPS: And more so, we need you to spread the word. Our fans are our best form of advertising! So, if you want to help us out, spread the word!

Thank you for reading our stories, and allowing us the opportunity to create characters you want to read again, and again ;-)

This holiday season will be a bit hard both because we are traveling a lot, and I lost someone in my family, so I'll be missing them this Christmas.

However, I'll spend a quiet time during the season to remember the good times. The times we laughed together, and the stupid things we would crack up about.

The smile on her face as we recounted things we had done in the past. The joy in her eyes when I took her to a nice restaurant.

Just her.

In my memories, she made the best chili I have ever had. She would mix Wick Fowlers spices plus some Gebhardt Chili powder, onions and canned tomatoes and I couldn't eat too much.

She wasn't perfect, not by a long shot but she was my mother. Who I am today was affected by her insights, her teachings, her screw-ups and her mistakes. None of us are perfect.

We are who we are.

So, this Christmas will be my first where one of my parents is no longer with me in person. But, I am so very happy to say that she will be with me in spirit, and memories.

Memories I will hold dear the rest of my life.

Ad Aeternitatem,

Michael Anderle

Sign up for Chris and Lee's newsletter for updates, new releases, and promotions. When you join the community, you'll get a FREE copy of their fast, fun thriller, *The Devil's Due:* https://www.subscribepage.com/chris_and_lee

Want more snarky heroines? Well, Chris and Lee also have an urban fantasy series about the mythic gods return to earth in their series with ST Branton, *Forgotten Gods.* The tagline is: *The gods are real, and they're assholes.* And it couldn't be closer to the truth. This series is fun, fast, exciting, and a little irreverent.

Vampires, werewolves, and all manner of monstrous creatures serve the unknown powers of old, but the story centers on the humans who make the heroic choice to fight them. Join Vic and her crew as they attempt to save earth from the gods who want it back. You won't forget, Forgotten Gods.

Oh, and… it is an 8 book omnibus almost always on sale for silly cheap!

While you're at it, we really thing you should try the new and improved *Steel City Heroes*:

A mad scientist fighting the laws of man and nature.

A demon-monster of mythical proportions.

A corporate conspiracy that goes back more than a century.

The Steel City is in desperate need of a hero.

Happy Reading!!

BOOKS BY MICHAEL ANDERLE

For a complete list of books by Michael Anderle, please visit:

www.lmbpn.com/ma-books/

All LMBPN Audiobooks are Available at Audible.com and iTunes

To see all LMBPN audiobooks, including those written by Michael Anderle please visit:

www.lmbpn.com/audible

www.ingramcontent.com/pod-product-compliance
Lightning Source LLC
Chambersburg PA
CBHW031623100726
47898CB00006B/1925